AFTERBURN

TIM CURRAN

1

Just before sunset, the sky went yellow and the air trembled like hot gelatin with not so much as a breeze. It was hot and humid and miserable. The barometer had been dropping for hours and at sundown, the storm made itself known as everyone knew it would on such a day. It came with a roaring wind that rushed through the town, stripping limbs from trees and shingles from roofs.

Then the rain began to fall across Middleburg.

It brought a chill that was welcome. The wind died and people ran out on porches and sidewalks to feel the temperature drop. They stood barefoot in the grass and on the cooling pavement, laughing as they reached hands up to the falling rain and felt it on their faces, truly comfortable for the first time in days.

Then something happened.

All of them felt it. It wasn't a tactile thing at first, but more of a suggestion that something was about to go exceedingly bad.

The rain, so joyously cool, turned hot.

Hot rain? It made no sense. Some weird atmospheric thing that wouldn't last, couldn't possibly last. But it did. It came down so hot it was almost searing.

Across the town, the rain-worshippers cried out and ran for cover, but very few made it. Most were trapped in it, confused and disoriented, the downpour scalding, steaming, and relentless. It got in their eyes, making them shriek in agony. It felt less like water and more like a fine liquid silicate, grinding beneath their lids like ground glass.

Very few were in any condition by then to see it, but the rain—if rain it was—came down in thick black sheets that ran like ink down faces, dying hair, and staining clothes.

And then something even worse happened.

The hot black rain evaporated and was replaced by a rumbling, dry downfall of meteoric dust particles that sounded like a deluge of sand hitting roofs and the walls of houses. The particles were nearly microscopic, cutting through clothing and flesh alike and for those trapped in them, the agony was exquisite and unbearable. It drove them to their knees, then laid them right out, twitching and writhing, bodies jerking with spastic tremors. Pierced by countless tiny particulates, brains short-circuited in skulls and bodies thrashed with scissoring limbs on the ground. Bladders voided, blood roared in veins, hearts hammered, and bleeding eyes rolled back in heads.

People screamed.

They vomited.

Blood gushed from their nostrils and ears, black bile bubbling between clenched teeth.

The fall of moondust lasted approximately twelve minutes and when it ceased, hundreds of people were laying in the streets and yards. Sick, burning up inside with what they knew not, abraded flesh shining with a curious metallic gleam, they crawled up onto porches and under trees, gasping out their last breaths, never realizing that they would never open their eyes again.

The dust dissipated and was replaced by a cool, easy shower that pattered on rooftops and beaded windows, washing the black liquid and faintly luminous dust from the streets. Then the storm ended and a dry wind blew through town. The heat spell had been broken, but something monstrous had taken its place.

2

About two hours after the storm had ceased, Abby Salter set aside her geometry text and checked her phone for messages. She cocked an ear, listening for the baby upstairs. The house was quiet. She turned up the monitor. It was silent up there, completely silent.

Good little Megan, she thought.

There were no texts or voicemails and she set her iPhone aside, yawning. Mr. and Mrs. Sumner said they wouldn't be home from Hazel Creek until at least two which gave her a couple hours to kill. What to do, what to do?

Sighing, she turned on the TV, sitting there in Mr. Sumner's recliner. She surfed the channels and found nothing interesting. For ten minutes she watched an infomercial on the Pocket Hose, something that always made her giggle. She grabbed her phone and called Kennedy then Polly, but neither answered. For a moment—a very fleeting sort of moment—she even considered calling David, but she decided against that. He hadn't called her in a week and there was no way in hell she was going act desperate and call him. He had her number—

What the hell is that?

She muted the TV and for a moment, there was nothing. She reached over and listened to the baby monitor. *All's quiet on the western front.* She turned the TV back up and right away, heard it again. She muted it.

A banging sound.

She got up. It was coming from outside. Next door or across the street. She parted the living room curtains and looked out there. Cupping her hands to the glass, she saw nothing interesting. The street was empty. The light at the corner reflected off dark pavement. Nothing moved out there.

She heard the sound again.

Next door?

She went into the kitchen and peered out at the Pearson house. She saw the hedges, the dew on the grass, the dark shape of the house itself. *Bang, bang, bang.* Ah, the screen door at the back porch wasn't latched. It was wide open, banging against the house. Mrs. Pearson was like in her nineties or something, Abby knew. She was a retired schoolteacher. Old, frail, she rarely left the house and only then to go to the doctor from time to time. Abby's mom had been one of her students way back in the day (which she often referred to as the Upper Cretaceous).

You should go shut that door. Go check on her.

Abby knew that was the right thing to do, but the idea didn't sit well on her. Besides, she was being paid to sit Megan and the Sumners wouldn't care for it much if she just abandoned her charge.

It'll only take a minute.

True, but what if something happened in that minute? That was the thing. Megan sounded like she was sleeping very deeply, but what if?

Megan was her mom's godchild which made her and Abby into like *godsisters* or something.

No, you need to stay here.

Abby turned up the TV again and right away she heard the door banging over there. Gah. It was going to drive her up the wall. She decided she would wait until the Sumners got home. Mr. Sumner could go take care of it then. That was the logical thing to do. *I was going to go shut it myself, Mr. Sumner, but I didn't want to leave Megan alone.* Yeah, that's what she'd tell them. They'd like that. It would mean she took her responsibilities seriously which was true. She had been babysitting for nearly two years now and her credentials were impeccable. This was something she took great pride in.

She flipped through the channels.

Crappy reality shows. Old movies. Sports. Nothing remotely grabbed her interest. Oh well, back to the infomercials. Wonder Wax. The Spin Mop. The Eggsercizer. The Potty Patch. She loved that one—it was a square of fake Astroturf-looking grass that your dog could take a dump on in the privacy of your own home.

Amazing.

And the grand thing—Abby liked the word *grand* because it sounded so...*grand*—was that it probably sold like crazy. There was someone out there getting rich so Pierre or Muffin or Princess

Poops-a-Lot wouldn't have to brave the nasty elements when he or she squeezed one out.

She wished Polly and Kennedy were there with her so they could laugh at some of this stuff. They particularly lost it over the products that just sounded wrong like the Wonder Nozzle, Ball Pets, and that absolute classic, the Pocket Fisherman.

If I do nothing else in this life, Abby thought, *I have to get involved in infomercials.*

She heard the door banging over there again and gritted her teeth. She knew she couldn't ignore it. She was far-too anal for anything like that. *Anal?* she could hear her mom saying. *My dear, you're so anal you're positively rectal.* Good one, mom.

"Isn't anyone else hearing this?" Abby said under her breath.

Screw it.

She went upstairs and turned on the hall light and peeked in on Megan. She was sleeping soundly. *I won't be long.* Abby went back downstairs and right away, she heard the door again. *Bang, bang, bang.* Gah! It was driving her nuts. She couldn't believe no one else was hearing it.

Another infomercial had started.

Sure, I'm gonna miss the Brazilian Butt Lift!

She put her boots and coat on and went back into the kitchen. She grabbed a magnetized flashlight from the side of the fridge. The wind nearly pulled the back door from her hand as she opened it. The damp chill settled into her right away as she stepped out onto the back porch. The night seemed impossibly dark and impossibly silent save the moaning wind.

Just get it done.

She moved down the steps and went through the gate that separated the Sumner yard from the Pearson's. The wind caught the gate, making it creak open and closed like the door of a haunted house. She quickly crossed the yard and went up the steps. The Pearson house was black and silent. As she took hold of the screen door she noticed that the inside door was open, too.

Now that was strange.

She clicked on the flashlight and played the beam over the inside door. There was a single black, sooty handprint on it that made her shiver. An awful stink was coming from inside the house…it smelled like burnt hair and something worse, something positively vile.

Abby stood there, uncertain what to do.

She knew the right thing—the thing her mom would expect of her—would be to go inside to see if old Mrs. Pearson was okay. That terrible smell was not normal in any way. But she couldn't leave Megan alone over there. That wasn't a good idea either.

And what if you go in there and the old lady is dead? Do you really want to see something like that?

She could call the police. Tell them…tell them something smelled funny next door? God, she was overreacting. She looked over at the Sumner house. She needed to get back.

But even so, she found herself stepping through the doorway into the Pearson house and whatever waited for her there.

3

At the end of the block, Patricia Reed waited for the police and, God knew, they were taking their sweetass time about it. Here she was, an old woman—well, seventy in two weeks—all by herself and they couldn't move their asses any faster than this.

For all they know, I've been raped and murdered, she thought. *Somebody might have come and chopped my head off.*

Well, if and when that happened, it would be on their souls. That was for sure. When somebody called for help, that meant they needed help. *Now.* Not twenty minutes later after a cup of joe and two cream-filled dainties.

Patricia had the lights off in the living room so she could see what was going on out there all that much better. What had concerned her initially was the slumped man. Some weirdo moving up the sidewalk, all slumped over, shambling unnaturally. Drunk or flying high on drugs, no doubt. That was bad enough. But when she heard the screams coming from the Tannebraughs next door, that's when she'd called.

Screams were a police matter.

She was too old to go over there and start poking into God only knew what. She thought of calling the Tannebraughs…but what if whoever was over there knew it was her and decided to come pay her a visit? A visit that would end in bloodshed, no doubt.

No, no, you did your civic duty. Let the professionals handle this.

Professionals? Oh God, she liked that. There were 5,000 people in Middleburg as of the last census (something she kept track of) and what police force they had was made up of local clowns who couldn't find their own assholes without a hand mirror and a well-greased finger. Why, last summer some drugged-up hophead had robbed the Rexall Drugs on Main Street. Not only robbed it, but held the employees at gunpoint. The police had responded, of course.

And what a sideshow that had been!

They showed up in black fatigues with dark grease smeared on their faces, running around like some half-ass SWAT team. Everyone on Main had gotten a good laugh at that. Little boys playing cop, pretending they were goddamn SEAL Team Six or some such crazy shit. Too many comic books and silly movies for those boys. They were some elite squad all right. The hophead had calmly walked out to his car and drove right past them. And they'd waved him through!

People were still laughing about that one. Calling the police Delta Farce behind their backs. And who could blame them? Oh, for the good old days when there were real cops and not these wannabees. All they cared about now was how cool and badass they looked. What an embarrassment. Back in the old days they had real cops like Buddy O'Neal and Frank Gerou. Frank would have cornholed these new toy cops and had them wearing dresses.

Oh, sure, but that's back when men were really men!

Oh, where the hell were they?

Maybe she'd better call again, light a fire under their asses. They'd probably stopped off at Marzetti's uptown for a thin crust or were still at the station posing in front of the mirror so they could see how cool they looked.

And why did it always have to be her? Why not the Kemps or the Sumners or the Brauns or the Shaws? Surely, they must have heard the screaming. She could give old lady Pearson a pass because she was deaf as a pine stump...but the others? How could they ignore these things?

And what about everyone across the alley? The Kultenbachs? The Zims? Old Bobby Pistera or even that evil bitch, Melody Marris? Did everyone have their damn ears shut off tonight?

Frustrated, disenfranchised, and disgruntled—three states which were practically a genetic inheritance in the Reed family like heart disease or alcoholism were in others—she mentally began writing another letter to the Middleburg *Press* on the inefficiency of the police.

Oh, had it been someone else who called, you could bet they'd be here by now. Like Melody Marris, for example. She with her bedroom eyes and long brown hair and longer legs. They'd have been here lickety-split for her, you could be certain of that. She was a private secretary and everyone knew what *that* meant. Patricia had little use for private secretaries in general because she figured they did their best work on their boss's laps and she had no use for Melody in particular because she had a Pro-Choice bumper sticker on her little red sports car (how many times had she spread her legs for that?) and proudly proclaimed to be an atheist. She even had one of those little metal Darwin fish on the back. All of which just went to show the kind of perfectly awful things that could happen when people started thinking for themselves.

People used to be burned for things like that, Patricia thought, *and maybe that wasn't such a bad idea.*

Wait. Okay.

Lights coming up King Street...*finally.* Here comes the pride of Middleburg. The patrol car stopped out in the street. Well, at least they had responded. That was something and Patricia figured she'd have to be content with that. She sighed and slid her cell phone back in her shirt pocket.

Why weren't they getting out of the car?

They were just sitting in there. The driver's side window unrolled and one of them looked up at her house.

Not here, dummy! Next door!

She knew what it was. They were just humoring her because...well, because maybe she did have kind of a habit of calling them a lot. But she never called without a very good reason.

She pressed her face closer to the glass until her nose touched.

They were probably going to walk up to the house, turn around and come knocking at her door. "Nope, nothing going on over there, ma'am."

Bullshit.

They had better do what they were getting paid for.

Maybe, just maybe mind you, she was willing to admit she'd called them out on a few fool's errands through the years, but this was the real thing. This one was serious as a heart attack and they had better not take it likely.

Something had happened over at the Tannebraughs. She didn't know what, but she had the feeling it was bad. Very, very bad.

4

Patricia Reed wasn't the only one who heard something. Across the street, Calvin Braun heard the screams in a vague, half-asleep sort of way and assumed it was kids running wild out there, up to no good. *Out tomcatting,* he thought sleepily as he opened his eyes. *Carry on like that, they're gonna get that wicked shrew Patty Reed all worked up.*

He looked over at the clock, but without his cheaters handy it could have been just about any old time. He tossed and turned for another ten minutes, started thinking about the pain he'd had in his chest that morning. Real bad pain that doubled him over. It lasted maybe five minutes and he thought he was a goner…then it just went away. He told himself all day it was just indigestion or acid reflux or something, but part of him did not believe that at all.

Now he was wide awake.

Next to him, Beth slept on like a fallen tree. When she was out, she was out. Not even thunder or a bomb going off could wake that woman.

Fuck it.

He got up and pulled on his lounging pants and went downstairs. He was too restless and worried. What he needed was a little something in his stomach. That would put him out and he'd sleep like a baby. They said not to eat at night because it turned to fat, but then they said a lot of things.

In the kitchen, he turned on the light and pawed around in the fridge. He found some cheddar cheese and a slab of ham. That would do it. In every old movie he'd ever seen, people always found a plate of fried chicken in the icebox for a midnight snack. Boy, he sure could have gone for some of that.

He sat down with a glass of milk and began slicing the ham and cheese into sticks. He took his time so that the rectangles were as uniform as possible. He didn't know why he did such things, but he found the very act somehow soothing. It drove Beth nuts. He cut his meat into perfect cubes, formed his mashed potatoes into ovals, lined up his string beans in perpendicular rows. To not do it made him feel edgy. He supposed a therapist would have had a field day with him.

But precision in life was important.

As he tasted his first stick of ham, he heard a rapping sound from somewhere and he wondered if Beth had forgotten to latch the back gate again. When he heard it for the second time, he knew it wasn't the gate; it was the front door.

What the hell?

Who'd be knocking this time of night?

He set his stick of ham aside, grabbed a swallow of milk, and walked out of the kitchen into the foyer. He heard the knocking again—slow, relentless, almost machinelike in its rhythm.

When someone knocked at your door in the dead of night, it only meant one of two things: there had been some sort of accident and the police had arrived to give you the bad news or some kids were out there raising hell. Cal smiled at the idea of the latter because he remembered doing things like that on Halloween night when he was a kid, sneaking out late and knocking on doors and then hiding. The idea of it made him smile momentarily, then frown as the knocking came again.

This wasn't Halloween.

What might have been acceptable that night was not acceptable tonight.

The knocking came again.

Bold little shits, ain't they? he thought.

He waited to see if they'd move on and pester someone else, but that goddamned knocking came again. Shit. Okay, all right. An unexplainable chill running down his spine like a caterpillar inching over the back of his neck, he reached out and threw the deadbolt, turning on the porch light at the same time.

Someone was standing out there.

He saw a dark shape as he fumbled in the pocket of his robe for his damn glasses. His hands were trembling as he put them on and saw what was standing there.

He took a step back, his skin crawling with gooseflesh, his heart fluttering in his chest.

It looked like a teenage boy.

One whose pallor was that of a corpse a week in the grave, bloodless and white, and he had no eyes…just ragged black pits. And his face…Jesus…there were holes in it, gaping holes the size of quarters.

A dummy, it's just a dummy.

The idea of that only calmed him slightly. A dummy with a fright mask. Sure. He looked around, searching for the perpetrators of this very unfunny prank. He saw no one and heard no giggling from the bushes.

What sort of sick fucking joke was this?

Well, he'd show them. He stepped out there. He'd toss that dummy out into the goddamn street. But close to it like that, his heart clenched in his chest and his hands shook at the idea of touching it.

They're trying to scare you.

Fuck that. He'd show 'em.

He reached out to push the dummy off the porch but as soon as his hand touched it, there was a searing pain. Goddamn thing was hot as a stove lid. Now how could that be?

Something was happening.

There was a hissing sound inside the thing and it began to shudder. Cal heard a crackling, popping sort of noise and smoke began issue from the dummy. It came from the holes in its face. From the eye sockets. The mouth opened and more smoke poured out as if it was boiling inside.

Cal took two fumbling steps backward and hit the floor. Something in chest went off like a clusterbomb and he gasped…and died.

By then, the lights were flickering and the dummy had stepped into the house. It moved past him, standing there at the foot of the steps, bubbling and sputtering like a cauldron of human grease. Then it started climbing the stairs, slowly, relentlessly. At the top it paused again.

It heard a voice: "Cal? Cal, is that you?"

That was all it needed. The voice drew it like a metal filing to a magnet. It sought the source and found it. Seconds later, Beth Braun screamed and there was a sound like breakfast links dropped onto a hot griddle.

Then there was only silence and an acrid, burnt stench that filled the house.

5

Patrolman Lane stepped out of the cruiser into the wind and shivered. What a night. What a first class clusterfuck of a night. The wind in his face and the chill crawling down his spine, he sighed and looked over at the Reed house. Even though the lights were off over there, he knew that Patricia was watching him. Face pressed up to the glass, she was studying his every move.

He waved.

She probably just flipped me off.

Lane adjusted the plastic bonnet atop his cap and moved up the walk to the Tannebraugh house. This was a waste of time and he knew it, but he'd see it through. All night long it had been that way. Crazy calls coming. People lying in the streets, sprawled on sidewalks, you name it. Reports of strange people out walking around. Screams. Gunfire.

Maybe it was this stinking weather.

Nothing would have surprised him tonight.

He walked up the porch steps. The house was dark. They were all probably sleeping and he was going to have to wake them up to satisfy Nosey Nora over there.

He peered through the window and could see shapes in there that were probably furniture and what not. Here goes. He knocked three times, violent, loud raps.

Waited.

He knocked again.

Come on, just wake up already. Come down here in your pajamas or nightgown and lay into me for waking you up.

But no one was coming. Not even when he hammered on the door until his fist was sore. He was starting to get a bad feeling about all this...after all, Old Lady Reed *had* reported screams. Could have been kids passing by. Could have been anything. Maybe the old bat imagined it. Then again, what if she hadn't?

Lane stood there.

Wish goddamn Jerry was here.

Jerry Teagan was his partner. Jerry was off the rest of the week because his wife was having knee surgery. Lane had always seen himself very much as the second banana of the team. Jerry had eight years on him. He always seemed to know what to do.

So what would he do right now?

But Lane knew. Jerry would call it in, then he'd try the doors. If one of them was open, he'd go right in. You needed probable cause to go barging into someone's house and screaming would have been all the probable cause Jerry would have needed.

Lane got on his Motorola walkie-talkie and called it in. That accomplished, he tried the door. It was open. All right then. He clicked on his flashlight and let himself in.

It was warm and dry inside…but there was a stench in the air that nearly curled his toes. A pungent, sickening odor that reminded him of burnt hair and possibly something even worse. He recognized the odor. When he was working his way through college in Chicago, he'd put in time at a slaughterhouse where the fats and blood were rendered in high temperature vats to be processed into bone meal. Once you'd smelled that stink, you'd never forget it.

And he was smelling it now.

Burnt hair.

Boiled fat and blood, steaming and rank in the air.

What the hell is going on here?

He tried to think of a reason for it, but he couldn't.

That bad feeling he had was perfectly awful by this point. His hand shook on the flashlight. His guts were churning, his mouth dry. He fumbled along the wall for a light switch and found one. *Click.* He was standing in an archway leading into a perfectly ordinary living room—sofa, recliner, computer desk, widescreen on the wall.

But as he stepped in there, the smell was stronger.

He went into the dining room, locating a light switch and flipping it on. He had to stop for a moment.

Dear God, that stink.

He pushed on through the dining room, bumping into a highboy with his knee, but completely oblivious to the pain. The stink was all he knew and the fear of what might have created it.

The kitchen.

The smell became even stronger.

Bile kicked up the back of his throat. His belly felt like it was filled with warm lard. There was a layer of steam near the ceiling. He was getting close now, too close. He saw dirty dishes in the sink, an empty can of beer, a pack of Winstons and a book of matches. Beyond the refrigerator, the room angled away out of sight. As he moved in that direction, he saw a black, glistening shape in the window and his heart caught in his chest.

It was his own reflection.

Oh brother.

He should have laughed. He should have at least smiled…but he found he could do neither. The tension inside him was tight as corset, squeezing his guts up into his chest cavity.

He put the flashlight in the pocket of his slicker and drew his Colt 9mm. His fingers were trembling on it. The gun felt like it was greased with Crisco.

He came around the side of the fridge and in the doorway leading out into the hall he saw something that made his eyes bulge from their sockets and his breath catch in his throat. He wasn't even sure what it was at first…just a prodigious amount of something like dripping wax that was splattered up the walls and dripping from the ceiling, gathering in an immense, steaming puddle on the floor. And twisted in that puddle was a set of bones with some shreds of clothing attached to them that looked charred as if they had been in a fire.

Even the bones were discolored. They looked like the fossils you see on TV…old, ancient, burnished a dull, unpleasant brown.

He stumbled into the refrigerator, making a gasping sound in his throat. The steam was gathering like mist in the air.

That was a person, a voice in the back of his mind whispered to him. *A person who had their flesh boiled from their bones.*

No, no, no. That was utterly inconceivable and what made it even more inconceivable was that it had happened right here, right in this fucking house in this perfectly Middle American neighborhood in good old Middleburg.

Lane, breathing very fast, hot/cold sweat beading his face, dug out his walkie-talkie and it slipped from his fingers. He heard it thump to the floor.

Shit.

The lights flickered.

Then they went out completely.

He had everything he could do not to scream like a terrified little girl. His stomach constricted and hot fingers of fear spread through his chest. He had never been afraid of the dark before, but at that moment every primal terror of the human condition had been unleashed in him.

He made a high whimpering sound in his throat, his hand reaching for his flashlight, finding it. It was like his fingers were numb. He could barely seem to hold the barrel of the light and working the on/off button seemed impossibly complicated as icy terror engulfed him.

There was a sudden flickering out in the hallway, subdued and irregular. A crackling sound like static electricity. He could feel his scalp get tight. The fine hairs at the back of his neck stood on end.

The flickering—sort of a weird blue-white strobing—was getting closer. Whatever was making it was coming up the hallway.

It was coming for him.

Lane backed up, his ass bumping into the kitchen table. He heard radio traffic on the walkie-talkie, but he didn't dare try to retrieve it. The energy was building as that ethereal flickering got closer. Any second now he would see what was making it.

He clicked on the flashlight.

The beam was bright at first, then it dimmed as if something in the atmosphere of the house was drawing the charge from the batteries. The beam dimmed to a spoke of yellow, then went out completely.

He heard the walkie-talkie die in mid squelch.

He dropped the flashlight, plucking his cell from his pocket. He would call in back-up, he would—

Jesus, the green display blinked and went out completely. It was fully charged. It couldn't happen.

This time he did scream as an impossible shape came through the doorway, reaching out smoking fingers to him like some wraith that had crawled blazing from a crematory pit.

He started shooting.

But it didn't do him a damn bit of good.

6

Another late-night pizza and a few more pounds of water weight to shed off, Candy Shaw thought as she closed the pizza box with a look of disgust on her face. She had lost sixteen pounds in the past two months on Weight Watchers and was actually starting to fit back into clothes she hadn't been able to wear in five years.

She was proud.

She felt empowered.

She felt invincible.

She honestly felt she could take on the world. Her biggest problem had always been the TV. As soon as it went on, the refrigerator door automatically opened. But for many months she had been free of that. Then she started binge-watching *Mad Men*, completely addicted. The first time she saw the commercial for Domino's deep-dish pizza, she ignored it. The second time, her mouth watered. Then, six or seven times later, she picked up the phone.

Now here she stood in the kitchen, sick to her stomach. She'd eaten half the damn thing and was just fraught with guilt. She wasn't going to tell Charlie. No, this little sin would be her dirty secret. Not that he would really care; he wasn't judgmental like that. Then again, he was thin and he didn't understand the battle of the bulge.

Feeling low with disgust but kind of excited at her sinful little secret, she took the pizza box and kitchen garbage out to the can in the alley. No one would ever know.

No one but you, dear, she thought. *Your own most unforgiving and nagging critic.*

It was funny, but she felt like some sort of closet drunk disposing of her empty bottles of booze in the dead of night. The rain had stopped anyway. She stuffed the pizza box in the can and put the kitchen garbage bag over the top. There. Securely hidden. Now where was the lid for the can? Ah, of course, sitting upside down atop the other can beneath the garage roof overhang. Charlie always did that. She grabbed it, realizing only at the last moment that there were tiny, glittering things in it as if someone had spilled a bag of gems.

"Ouch! *Jesus!*" she cried as she dumped them and they fell over her bare legs like loose sand. They were not only hot, almost scalding—something which was freakish—but they adhered to her, gluing right to her skin. She dropped the lid and tried to brush them away, but somehow they had pierced her skin and disappeared beneath it like they were living things, tiny tunneling insects.

Before she could even process what that might mean, waves of agony doubled her over, forcing her down to her knees. She screamed in a broken voice that soon became a gurgling as she rolled in the grass, bolts of agony drilling into her. It felt like everything inside her was twisting like a hot screw. She vomited. She gagged. She contorted with seizures as her brain went haywire. It felt as if every organ in her body was swelling like rotting fruit on a vine. Her brain felt too big for her skull and her eyes burned like someone had dumped acid in them.

Oh God oh Jesus the pain the FUCKING PAIN!!!

She blacked out for a few minutes and when consciousness returned, it was dreamlike and vague. The blood in her veins seemed hot and bubbling. The agony wasn't so bad now. It had been replaced by a numbness that made her body feel like it had been poured from rubber.

Something had changed.

Something had shifted.

Something inside her was being remade.

She did not understand and she couldn't understand, only that whatever it was it was going full bore inside her, replacing that curious numbness with devastating waves of agony that were even worse than before.

She crawled through the grass like a road-struck dog, whimpering, coughing out gray ribbons of saliva and clouds of warm vapor.

She tried to call for help, but she had no voice. The only thing that would come out of her was a croaking sort of noise. Her mouth felt hot as fireplace soot and just about as dry. As she tried to moisturize it, her tongue ran over her gums and her teeth began falling out. She gagged them out along with silvery ropes of bile that glistened and gleamed in the grass, breaking up into shiny beads like liquid mercury.

And her eyes…

They were huge in their sockets, bulging like boiled eggs, the irises no longer a dazzling Nordic blue but bleached to a sallow yellow, the corneas like veils of purple-red starshot. They were pulsating like the hearts of toads. She screeched with a strident cry of pain as she felt something like hot pins in them, pressing in deeper and deeper.

And it was about that time that blood began to bubble from her scalp in scarlet freshets that streaked down her face and clumped her hair in red tangles. Her eyes continued to pulsate wildly, swelling, oozing a serous fluid that hissed as it combined with the blood on her face.

She tried to scream one last time but there was nothing left to scream *with*. Her vocal cords were burned out, her throat hot as a chimney pipe. Her eyes superheated and boiled from their sockets, steaming and sputtering.

But thankfully, she was out cold by then.

Maybe not even truly still alive in the accepted sense. Wisps of steam rose from her pores and fingers of cold blue current ran up and down her body.

Sometime later, beneath the pale lunatic eye of the moon, she began to move.

7

Like Patrolman Lane, Abby, much against her better judgment, entered the Pearson house, smelling that awful cremated stink and it stopped her dead. Did she continue on or did she call the police? The smell was not normal. Nobody had burnt a pizza or left the popcorn in the microwave too long.

This was beyond an ordinary odor.

It was almost…violent, if that made any sense.

But she had come this far. Maybe Mrs. Pearson needed help. Maybe the house was on fire.

Burning houses do not smell like this. Stinks in here like somebody roasted a dog, hair and all.

She had to steady herself so as not to let her stomach get the best of her. It very badly wanted to crawl right up the back of her throat. Leading herself forward by flashlight, Abby searched the walls until she found a light switch.

There. That was better.

There was a short set of steps leading up into the house and another that went down to the basement. She wasn't about to go down there. A quick little trip into the house, a ten second look around and then she was out of there. She wasn't being paid to babysit Mrs. Pearson.

Up the steps into the kitchen. It was small, neat, very orderly. Not a dirty dish to be found. The countertops were gleaming and the stainless steel sink was shining. It looked like it was never even used. The thing, of course, that caught Abby's eye was the lone gadget on the counter near the oven. It was a Wraptastic cling film dispenser. She loved that infomercial. It was the one where the lady was trying to wrap up some meat with ordinary Saran Wrap and she got tangled up in it and—

Knock it off for godsake.

Yes, she wasn't here for this. In fact, she wasn't really sure why she was here at all. This was practically home invasion.

But the open door.

That awful stink.

Something had happened here and she could not make herself believe it wasn't something really, really bad. She stepped through the kitchen and stopped at a short hallway beyond.

"Mrs. Pearson? You okay?" she called out, feeling entirely foolish. "Mrs. Pearson, it's me, Abby Salter from next door. I'm watching Megan for the Sumners."

Why don't you just give her your entire life story?

Abby sighed. She was tempted to call out again, but there was something about her voice echoing out into that dead silence that unnerved her. She needed to get out of there right now. Panic was rising in her and she could not control it. She told herself that she didn't belong there. That if Mrs. Pearson came downstairs and found her there she'd probably have a freaking heart attack.

But the real reason that she started backing away to leave was that she was scared. She couldn't explain it, but it was there…a finger of dread worming inside her.

As she got to the door to quickly jog down the steps and back out into the night, she heard a thumping upstairs like somebody had bumped into a wall. Something else crashed up there and she jumped.

Either leave or go see what this is about.

She turned to leave, heard another thumping, and turned to investigate. She knew it was a bad idea and every fiber of her being cried out for her to get back to the Sumner house while she still could. But the morality that her mother had pounded into her head year after year would not let her abandon someone in need.

Quickly then, before she had time to properly think it over, she crossed the kitchen and into the hall. She couldn't find a light out there, so she followed the wall until she found the stairs. There. A light switch. She clicked it on and breathed a bit easier when the shadows were chased out of the stairwell.

She climbed up three steps, stopped. The second stair creaked so loudly it made her breath catch in her lungs. That stink was getting stronger now. "Mrs. Pearson?" she called out. "Hey, Mrs. Pearson! It's Abby Salter…your door was wide open. You okay?"

She heard a faint sound from above. A subtle sort of movement that repeated itself again and again.

She climbed up three more stairs. The landing above was a well of darkness. Images passed through her head from every slasher movie she'd ever seen, telling her that someone was probably waiting for her up there.

But that was ridiculous.

"Mrs. Pearson?" she called out, her voice noticeably weaker now. It was just above a whisper and she wasn't even aware of the fact.

She stopped.

She'd heard a voice…a weak, rasping sort of sound.

"Mrs. Pearson?"

Feeling truly scared now, her skin covered in goosebumps, she forced herself up to the top. Now she could hear that regular, repeated sound. It was sort of a creaking. *Creak, creak, creak.* Was it a bed? She shook certain ideas from her head that would make a bed creak. That was absurd.

At the top of the stairs, her heart fluttering in her chest, she looked vainly around for a light switch.

Creak, creak, creak.

It was so steady, so regular…like the sound a machine might make. Maybe that's what it was. Mrs. Pearson was old. Maybe she had one of those breathing machines old people used sometimes. The idea of that relieved her somewhat, but the gathering stink brought the fear back again, white and hot in her belly.

The creaking continued.

She followed it to its source. It was coming from an open doorway at the end. She was sure of it. Now it was only a matter of going down there and seeing what this was all about. Even as her instincts told her quite clearly to turn and run, she moved forward with the flashlight held out before her, the beam unsteady in her trembling hand.

Creak, creak, creak.

The very sound set her nerves on edge. Her breath was coming very fast now. She reached the doorway and said, "Mrs. Pearson?" in a low, almost pained sort of voice. The creaking continued unabated. She heard that voice again…that garbled, rasping voice.

She shined the light into the room as her other hand reached for the light switch. She saw a form in a chair, rocking back and forth, back and forth. It was distorted somehow, unnatural. Her fingers found the light switch and a lamp on the other side of the room came on.

Abby led out a strangled cry because she did not know what that grotesque thing was.

It could have been Mrs. Pearson.

It could have been a lot of things.

It was roughly human in shape, a nodding form that was blackened and crumbling, plumes of oily smoke rising from it. It had cracked open in places like parched earth, a down of gray ash settled on the floor around it and over the arms of the rocker. A slit in the face opened and that horrible rasping voice spoke. And as it did so, it exhaled a cloud of gray soot.

"Help me…" it said. *"Help me…"*

It lifted a smoking stick of an arm up, the brittle fingers breaking away and striking the floor where they burst open with puffs of ash. Then the entire body caved in like there was nothing inside it. It collapsed into itself and Abby could see the rungs of bones beneath.

She was beyond ordinary fear by that point.

The sight of the thing and the acrid stink it gave off made her reel with dizziness. She was hanging onto the doorframe so she didn't pitch right over.

The thing that had been Mrs. Pearson looked like a heap of gray cigar ash with bones protruding from it, a gape-jawed burnt skull grinning with morbid delight.

There was a scream in Abby's throat that wanted to get free, but she didn't let it.

Because there was another creaking sound.

She heard it quite distinctly. Not the rocking chair this time. It came from below and she knew with a horrid, sinking feeling that it was the second step on the staircase.

Somebody was coming up the stairs.

The light in the room began to dim.

She looked out towards the stairwell. The lights below were dimming, too. And just before they went out completely, she saw a monstrous shadow played over the wall, a hideous creeping form.

Then there was darkness.

8

What in the name of Pete was going on over there?

Patricia Reed, of course, still had her nose to the glass of the living room window as she did most every day and many nights. She saw the cop get out and go to the front door of the Tannebraugh house. She heard him knocking, then he went in after waiting out there an interminably long time.

She knew it was that little shit Dennis Lane. He'd been nothing but a spoiled little brat and a troublemaker as a kid and now he was a cop. An idiot like that with a badge was like a blind man with a chainsaw in a crowded room.

No matter.

He went in and she saw lights go on. Good, good. He was getting to the heart of the matter then. Now she was waiting, nose against the glass. Well? *Well?* What was happening over there? What had he found? Was he just going to stand around in there or was he going to get some backup over here?

Dammit!

The tension and suspense were almost more than she could take. But she had to calm down. She was no young thing anymore and all that excitement wasn't good for her.

But how could she calm down?

"Come on, you clown," she said. "What's going on over there?"

Then she saw…what was this?

The lights over there were going out, dimming down to nothing. That made no sense. That's not how the power went out. It didn't get weaker. It was like one of those dimming switches was being used over there, slowly being turned down. What was that imbecile doing over there? Playing with the lights? Why couldn't they send a real cop over here? God, they had to have at least one. Even a greasy, well-thumbed deck of cards held one shiny ace.

She saw flashes of light.

What in the hell?

Yes, on and off, on and off...a sort of blue-white phosphorescence, an irregular guttering sort of light. Then she clearly heard a scream and nearly fell off the couch. Shots were fired. They were clear and sharp like the banging of a snare drum.

Patricia, terrified now, every inch of her body alive and shuddering, stumbled over to the phone.

Oh God, oh God.

Whoever was over there was either dead on the floor from Dennis Lane's bullets or *he* was on the floor. And if it was the latter then quite possibly the killers over there would be coming for her next.

As she fumbled her cell from her shirt pocket, nearly dropping it twice, a wild and shocking train of thought occurred to her: *Maybe that's what this is about. Killers. Cold-blooded killers. They're going from house to house to house, slaughtering everyone they find...*

She punched in 911 on the cell. It connected almost immediately and she got a voice recording that told her all operators were currently busy...then there was an eruption of static on the line and an odd sort of whining like a radio that couldn't quite bring in a station.

She saw that flickering light outside.

It was there and then it was gone like a switch being thrown.

They're coming for you! They're right outside!

Yes, that was the same sort of light she'd seen right before Dennis Lane—or whom she assumed was Dennis Lane—screamed and started shooting. Her entire body trembling, Patricia tried 911 again but there was only static. She tried to flick on the lamp on the table, but it was dead.

Everything was dead.

Dead as you'll soon be if you don't—

There was a knocking at the front door, slow, steady—*boom, boom, boom.*

She nearly fell over with panic. The door was locked. In fact, all the doors were locked as were the windows. There was no way they could get in, absolutely no way. The cell was still in her hand and she dialed 911 but, again, got nothing but static.

She kept trying.

Oh, please...oh dear God, please.

Her entire body was shaking now. She was too old for this. She didn't have a gun. She didn't have anything. On her hands and knees now, debilitated by a raw terror that was so immense it threatened to crush her, she crawled unsteadily over to the fireplace. She tried to pull a brass poker from the rack and the whole thing spilled, clattering noisily.

Now they know! If they didn't know before, now they know you're hiding in here!

She huddled there in the shadows, nearly hyperventilating. Her head swam with dizziness. Her hands were greasy with sweat and she could barely hold onto the poker. In her chest, her heart banged away, barely keeping its rhythm. Now and again, it would miss a beat and a jolt of pain would shoot right up into her neck.

Boom, boom, boom.

She was on her own now and she knew it. Even the police she had criticized so severely through the years could not help her nor could the neighbors she had condemned and tormented. She was alone as perhaps she had always been. A woman teetering on old age, defenseless and vulnerable.

If she wanted to survive this, she would have to take some kind of action.

She pulled herself to her feet, her stomach rolling over with nausea from being flooded with adrenaline. She pulled herself along the wall until she reached the double doors that opened to the entry. She peered through the crack and...*oh my dear sweet Jesus*...she saw a hulking dark figure outside on the porch. It was a vague, amorphous shape peering through the window set in the door. Only the sheer curtains hid it from her in detail.

Boom, boom, boom.

The knocking was followed by that eerie flickering again and for one terrible moment she saw what was out there...it was almost as if it had been x-rayed.

She had to bite down on her lower lip so that she did not scream. Carefully then, she closed the double doors and hoped beyond hope that the shadows hid her actions. When the doors were shut, she locked them. Then she backed through the living room. She would lock every door between her and what waited out there.

There was no more knocking for a few moments. Maybe *it* had gone away—by this time she was no longer believing that what stood on the porch was strictly human as such. Then there was a crackling sound like electricity arcing from a downed power line and she heard the door crash in. Not just open, but crash as if it had been blown right off its hinges.

She backed away frantically, her heart skipping in her chest. She saw a pulsating blue light just beneath the double doors. Then there was a popping sound like a fuse had blown. The knobs of the doors and the lock itself glowed and fell from their housing, the wood around them blackened and smoking.

The doors swung open.

Screaming and hysterical, Patricia tried to get away. She made it into the kitchen, bumping into walls and furniture in the dark and the shape came for her. She smelled a stink like burned wiring and heard a strange sizzling sound. As she reached for the door leading down into the cellar, a hand grabbed her by the shoulder and everything inside her began to blaze and she slumped, smoldering, to the floor.

Her skeletal fingers still gripped the lump of melted plastic that had once been her cell phone.

9

When Charlie Shaw was a kid back in the much-loved, long-gone 1970s, all the scrubs in the neighborhood would get together on summer nights and play a game called Statues while moths winged about the streetlights. The point was to freeze yourself in the position of whatever it was you were trying to imitate and let the guesser try and figure out what you were. You might hunch down low with bared teeth and fingers outstretched like claws in imitation of a lion or stand tall with a grim look on your face and stiff outstretched arms if you were Frankenstein's monster. It was a fun game and they always had lots of good laughs on those warm, well-remembered evenings.

He figured kids probably didn't play backyard games like that anymore. Now they had laptops and tablets and smartphones to pass the time. The age of imagination and simple fun like Statues was extinct.

So, when he pulled onto Wishbone Avenue about two blocks from his house, nobody was more surprised than him to see well over a dozen people playing the game.

Except, they weren't kids.

They were adults.

What in the fuck is this now? he wondered.

He slowed his pickup to a crawl and looked at the people standing out on lawns and sidewalks frozen stiff as boards. They were like statues in a park waiting for pigeons to shit on them.

Was it some kind of gag?

Some kind of game?

He drove on past but his curiosity got the better of him by the time he reached the intersection of Wishbone and Marble Heights. He pulled a U-turn and drove straight back there, this time turning on the high beams so he could see just what in the Christ this was about.

When he reached the area of the statues—he didn't know what else to call them—he stopped and just watched them. None of them moved. Hell, they didn't even flinch. He pulled a cigarette from his pack of Winstons and fired it up.

"Well, this fucking beats all," he said to himself.

He wondered if anyone else was seeing this, but the houses on both sides of Wishbone were just as dark and silent as graveyard tombs.

He saw men and women. Some were dressed and some were not. That was the perfectly obscene and disturbing thing—several of them were naked.

He waited there, idling.

Did he look into this or call the cops? Or did he just go on his way and mind his own business?

There's something seriously fucked-up and scary about this, he heard a voice in his head say. *Just get out of here.*

That was instinct and common sense sharing a single voice and some very sage advice. But Charlie rarely paid much mind to things like inner voices and gut instinct, so he stepped out of the pickup and walked over to a man standing there in a bathrobe.

The guy didn't have any eyes.

It was crazy but there was nothing but black holes in his face. Charlie felt cold fear settle into him. This just wasn't right. As he walked about, he saw that none of them had eyes. He stumbled back, nearly tripping over a tall, buxom blonde woman whose naked skin was the color of porcelain, though mottled by dark contusions. Like the others, there were what looked like ragged chasms in her flesh and face as if some kind of tropical ulcers had eaten holes in her.

A disease, he thought then. *They all got some kind of disease.*

He slowly backed towards the pickup, crying out when the forgotten cigarette in his hand burned his fingers. He tossed it. "Shit," he said.

He wished dearly then that he owned a cellphone. Candy had one. She was always after him to get one, but he hated the damn things only slightly more than he hated the assholes who were always glued to them. People driving and talking, totally distracted, cutting off other drivers. Damn things ringing off in restaurants and theaters, annoying the shit out of everyone. Funny how the world survived so long without them.

Too bad he didn't have one of those stupid things now because he would have called the cops. Somebody had to be made aware of this.

Right now, though, getting out of there before he picked up whatever they had was of primary importance. He jumped back in the cab and right away the headlights dimmed and the dashboard lights flickered.

The truck died right there in the middle of the street. *Fucking Chevies,* he thought. *Fucking junk.* What a time to let him down. He pulled a flashlight out of the glovie, but the batteries were dead. Dammit. He popped the hood and hopped out. The hood gave a great grinding creak as it went up. Just about loud enough in the stillness of night to wake the dead of three counties.

Now that's a hell of a thing to be thinking.

Because, really, these people did look like they were dead and the idea of them all waking up at once was more than a little frightening.

Oh boy.

Something was going on. It was as if his fear had been read and made real. The statue people were trembling, limbs jerking. They made sizzling sounds like burning cigarettes dropped into puddles. *Sssssssttt.*

They were *burning.*

He saw it with his own eyes, his heart pumping painfully, and he still didn't believe it. Smoke was coming out of them, hissing from them like their guts were on fire. It rose up in plumes, the breeze gradually dissipating it. The smell of it was much like boiling battery acid, bitter and hot.

The people were moving.

No, no, no, don't do that, the voice in his head said. *Just stay put...please just stay put...*

But they weren't staying put.

"You people," he said. "Just stay where you are! I'll get you some help!"

As if drawn by his voice, they turned in his direction and slowly shambled towards him like extras in a George Romero movie...except these extras were sizzling and smoking, pouring out gagging fumes in churning contrails as they came on.

They were bearing down on him.

He stumbled away from the truck, his insides knotted with terror. Like some dumb girl in a horror movie, he tripped over the curb and his ass hit the grass. He was struck numb by it all. He opened his mouth to scream, but nothing came out.

And that was a good thing he realized seconds later. The people were moving around, blind as moles, reaching out with fingers that sizzled and popped like burning twigs, tendrils of smoke rising from them.

They were at the pickup, putting their hands on it, seemingly unaware that he was no longer there, feeling around for him.

They didn't know where he was.

That was the thing.

The groaning creak of the hood is what seemed to have activated them. Being blind as stones, they were hunting by sound. He watched them pressing their hands on the truck, inside and out. They left burned black handprints in the paint. In fact, the paint had actually *run* in spots as if their hands were red-hot pokers.

Charlie didn't need any more convincing.

If he was quiet, they wouldn't be able to find him.

Silently, trying to control his gasping breath, he stood up and moved slowly across the lawn to the sidewalk. They still hadn't heard him. Good. Without further ado and despite his fifty years, he ran like hell.

10

"It'll just take us ten minutes," Joe Sumner said, pulling his VW up to the gas pump at the Amoco just outside Middleburg. "We don't get some fuel in this baby, we'll be lucky to coast home."

Susan nodded, but he could see that she was tense. She'd been trying to call home for the past fifteen minutes and Abby just wasn't answering the phone. It probably meant nothing. But like most new moms, she fretted constantly.

"I don't like this," she said.

"I'll be quick," he promised her.

The good thing was that he was the only one at the pumps. The bad thing was that the pump he'd pulled up to had a damaged credit card slot which meant he'd have to go in and pay. No big deal, but it all took time.

As he filled the VW's tank, he saw Susan on the phone again. He already told her it wouldn't do her much good, but she wasn't one to listen. Either one of two things had happened—lines were down from the storm or the internet had crashed again. They had their cable, internet, and phone bundled through Charter and rarely was there a day when those bozos didn't drop the ball. It was almost a given that two, three hours daily there would be no internet.

It was time to switch providers.

He watched the digital display of the pump and it seemed to be taking forever. Good God. He could almost feel Susan's tension coming from inside the car or maybe it was his own. There was no reason for it. Abby was a good sitter, very reliable. Megan was in good hands.

The best, he thought.

At sixteen Megan already had two solid years of babysitting under her belt and knew a hell of a lot more about little ones than either Susan or he did. Her references were impeccable. Besides, her mother was an RN and lived two or three blocks away. What better set-up was there than that?

Finally, the tank was full.

He opened the door and grabbed his wallet off the dash. "Just be a sec."

Susan nodded tersely.

"Why don't you call your sister?" Joe suggested. "See if her phone is out, too."

Susan brightened. "Good idea."

The voice of a little boy inside him wanted to say, *women.* The way Spanky used to say it in Our Gang comedies when he was frustrated with Darla or his mother back in the day. Ordinarily, this would have made him smile...but he was not smiling because he was starting to feel a species of nameless anxiety working its way through him a bit at a time. Maybe he had picked it up from Susan. Maybe her parental fears were catchy. Regardless, as he crossed the lot to the gleaming bright station, he began to feel terribly afraid and he did not know why.

There was no reason, but it seemed to be getting stronger.

Strong enough that he paused six feet from the sliding glass doors, looking at all the displays piled in the windows—Kingsford charcoal, Pennzoil, Lays potato chips, Gatorade—and feeling a dread that he simply could not put a name to.

As the doors slid open to receive him, he felt a sort of irrational fear gather in his chest.

And as he stepped inside, a smell hit him.

He couldn't even be sure what it was. He only knew it did not belong. A foul stench of things burned and blackened that seemed to crawl down his throat and stir his stomach. It was possible a deep fryer or something had malfunctioned, but he didn't believe it.

This is how a plague pit must have smelled, he mused uneasily. *When they dumped bodies infected with the Black Death into a big hole and lit them up.*

But again, this was irrational and groundless.

He stepped further inside, passing stacked cases of Icehouse and Sam Adams, Lipton Green Tea and bottled water. Everything seemed perfectly fine other than that horrendous smell which hung like vapor in the air and the fact that the place seemed to be empty. Completely empty.

"Hello," he said, disturbed by how his voice died in the stillness like a pebble dropped into a deep dark pond.

He walked slowly past the counter which seemed to have sprouted canisters of Slim Jims and Sasquatch beef jerky. There were racks of cigarettes, a chromium-edged ice cream cooler, row after row of glass-fronted freezers, aisles of junk food. It looked identical to every convenience store in the country, save there were no people.

He stepped around the counter and discovered that he was wrong.

Way down at the end, sprawled in the doorway leading into a storeroom was something that looked almost like a person. At least, it had arms and legs.

That's...that's not real, Joe. I mean, shit, look at it. Looks like something from Madame Tussauds' that somebody left under a fucking heat lamp.

Yes, that's exactly what it looked like...but he had a very nasty feeling that this was no dummy, no gag, no goddamn prank. Because wax or latex didn't smell like this.

He was practically choking on the stink.

He stepped carefully towards the grisly remains, trembling, trying to make sense of what he was seeing. This thing was simply far too realistic to be some cheap gag made of plastic and petroleum jelly.

He only dared get within ten feet of the thing because the odor was so strong. Tendrils of steam were rising from it. What he saw there on the floor was a badly-used skeleton caught in a pool of goo like melted cheese, only it wasn't cheese and he knew it.

What kind of heat would that take? a small voice in the back of his head wondered. *How much heat would it take to liquefy the flesh of a human being and char the skeleton beneath?*

Maybe that wasn't something he wanted to know. He began slowly backing up, looking around the entire time as if maybe he expected that a camera would be rolling to capture his reaction to this oh-so unfunny prank. But he saw no cameras, save the typical surveillance cam on the ceiling. All he saw was the empty store to one side and to the other, out the window, his lone VW at the pumps with the dark form of his wife waiting for him.

Joe wasn't a guy who scared easily and up until that point, he didn't think he'd honestly, truly been scared his entire adult life. But he was scared now. His heart was pumping manically like he'd just ran two block at full sprint. His breath seemed to rasp in his lungs as if they were having a hell of time extracting any good breathable oxygen from the surrounding air. His muscles were bunched, his nerves strung tight like violin strings, and an itchy sort of heat had spread up his belly and over his chest. He had the worst feeling that if he didn't get a grip on things, he was going to pass right out.

You're not going to pass out, he told himself. *There's no time for fucking theatrics. Whatever happened here is serious business and you're going to do something about it and you're going to do that right now, understand?*

He understood, all right. He dug his cell out with trembling fingers and dialed 911. He got through, but was put on hold. *All operators are currently busy, please hold.* What the hell was that about? Since when did 911 put you on fucking hold? What was going on here?

He heard footsteps behind him.

"You should have gotten out while you still could," a voice said.

11

Earl Kressup had a secret and he kept that secret deep in his heart where no one could ever find it. The secret lived in there, alive and scurrying, multi-legged and perniciously active. Some days over at the school as he mopped the floors or cleaned the Girl's bathrooms or just loitered about in the hallways (pretending he was doing a bit of maintenance on the radiators, heh heh), the secret would get very excited. It would make him tremble and sweat as it raced around inside him. Much like the steam system that heated the school, it needed to be bled from time to time. Otherwise it would get out of control.

When he thought about the Secret—which was without a doubt a full-blown obsession which deserved proper noun status— and started to feel dirty inside, his conscience rising into the full bloom of guilt, he liked to think of Bob Crane. Crane was the guy who played Hogan on *Hogan's Heroes* and had his own little dark secret that came out after his death. Crane had hinted around about it more than once by saying, "I don't drink. I don't smoke. Two out of three ain't bad."

And that's the way Earl looked at things.

Maybe what he did might be smarmy to some, but there were worse things. There were always worse things in this world.

Why do you even think about it?

He didn't know. Maybe because he had gone to Catholic school and bought into the guilt trip they brainwashed him with. Maybe that was part of it.

As things slowly escalated out of control in Middleburg (something he was ignorant of), he tossed and turned in his bed, thinking about things he told himself he must not think about. He was doing it too much and that wasn't good.

But it's there. It's waiting for you.

No!

Why not? What better time to go collect what's yours and yours alone?

There was a twisted logic to that.

The Secret inside perked up its ears, getting randy and agitated. Earl imagined he could actually hear it breathing faster and faster, feel its hot breath blowing up the back of his throat. It began to claw at his insides, making hot blood run down into lower regions.

I can't go over to the school in the middle of the night. For godsake, how would that look? What if someone caught me there? How the hell could I explain myself?

The Secret laughed its evil little laugh. What was there to explain? He was chief custodian. He popped in to check the boilers. He overhauled a leaky boiler valve and he was keeping an eye on it for leaks. It was a matter of safety. Who could possibly question that?

Hmm.

That was plausible. In fact, it sounded pretty damn good. No…no, he was going back to sleep. He couldn't be getting this obsessed. It wasn't healthy. He closed his eyes, breathed in and out, and tried to relax. Dear God, it was just no good! He couldn't sleep! He couldn't relax! Not with what was waiting for him at the school!

The Secret was raging inside of him.

It was growling.

It was slavering.

It was shrieking its hunger into the night.

Without really thinking about it, moving now pretty much on autopilot, he pulled his green work pants on and a t-shirt. He went downstairs and climbed into his boots and black rain slicker.

Just doing my job, he told himself. *I'm just doing my job.*

It wasn't true.

It wasn't true at all.

There were holes in the lies that had formed in his head. If he suspected a boiler leak, then why hadn't he informed school administration? There was a safety protocol outlined by the state. Why hadn't he initiated any of it?

Ten minutes later, he was pulling into the back parking lot of Middleburg High school. He sat there for a time in his pickup, trying to build up the will to drive away. But the Secret beckoned. The Secret needed to be satisfied. It was growing increasingly unruly. If he didn't satisfy it, why, it might prod him into darker activities and he couldn't have that.

Pulling off a Lark Full Flavor Red, his hand trembling, he said in a low, wounded-sounding voice, "I'm in charge here. I'll decide what I do and what I don't do. That's the way it fucking is."

Inside, he could hear the sardonic laughter of the Secret. It was the laughter of a child molester heard in a lonely wood: braying, cold, inhuman.

Oh, you will, will you? Let's get something straight, dumbass, shall we? You're a middle-aged, unmarried freako that likes to watch naked teenage girls while he pulls on his dick. You think that's healthy and normal? WRONG, monkeyskull! WRONG! It ain't normal and neither are you. I'm what hatched from the egg you mothered over. You been feeding me and stroking me and protecting me for years. Don't you even think of cutting me off or I'll make you do things that would make a cop fucking puke!

Get it?

With guys like you it starts by watching.

But it don't take much to turn it into something else, now do it? No sir. It's just video now, but I can give you obsessions beyond just watching. You cut me off and a week from now you'll have one of those leggy girls wrapped in a tarp in your basement.

Do you get it?

Am I coming in clear?

Earl whimpered and dropped his cigarette. He put his hands over his face. Tears leaked between his fingers. The Secret owned him. It knew all about him and if he didn't do what it said...oh, God, it would be unspeakable. At the very least it would make him fuck up, make him make a mistake and be exposed for what he was.

He couldn't have that.

He just couldn't.

"I'll go get it," he said, picking up his cigarette. "I will. I'll do it right now."

So move it, perv.

The Secret wasn't fucking around now; it meant business. It forced Earl's hands down between his legs. It made him unzip his pants and free his erection. It made him stroke himself as his eyes

rolled in their sockets with ecstasy. The Secret moaned inside him.
Yes, *yes,* that was how the game was played. That was the name of
the fucking tune. That's how the bear slept in the woods and the
farmer scythed the wheat.

Easy, easy, not just yet!

Trying to control himself, Earl took long slow drags off his
coffin nail, thinking about the school, thinking about warms days
when the sweat beaded his brow and he trembled sickly like a
shivering puppy watching those teenage girls with their short skirts
and long legs, their firm little titties straining against their tight
tees. How many times had he ducked into the boiler room or the
janitor's hutch out of sheer embarrassment, his erection standing
hard like a tent pole in his pants? How many times had he hid
away, the Secret breathing hot and heavy in his ears, a sharp-
smelling sweat dampening his shirt, just so he could masturbate?

The Secret giggled at that. *Sick little perv,* it said. *If those
parents ever found out how you lust after their daughters...how
you'd like to ram into their tight little fucktwats until the honey ran
hot and pure, your fingers tightening around their throats,
squeezing, squeezing until their faces went purple-blue and their
eyes bugged from their heads...oh, they'd kill you!*

Stop it.

He had to stop thinking like that. It was wrong. It was
obscene. It was unnatural, it was—

Delicious.

Earl finished his cigarette and tossed it out the window. He
started the pickup. He was going to drive away. It was the right
thing to do and he would do it. He wasn't about to be broken on
the wheel of guilt and criminal desire by some stinking, silly little
voice inside his head—

Shut the fucking truck off, you simpering little maggot.

"No!"

Do it or I'll make things unpleasant for you.

"I refuse!"

*Do you? Do you really? Well, ain't that the shits. If you refuse
that leaves me out in the cold. Boo-hoo. But I won't be out here
alone, you little fucking pervert. You'll be with me. Tomorrow
night there's going to be a town hall meeting at the school.*

Parents'll be there, teachers, administration, even the school board itself.

"Please," he mumbled.

You'll be in attendance, too. Approximately twenty minutes into the meeting, you will walk up front, unzip your pants, and begin masturbating in front of everyone. All the—

"NO! NO! NO!"

All the while, you'll be raving to the parents about how you watch their daughters! How you want to fuck them and bite them and suck them and strangle the very fucking life out of them so you can have their cold, cold corpses to—

"SHUT UP! YOU BETTER SHUT THE HELL UP! DO YOU FUCKING HEAR ME?"

Easy, Earl. I'm just toying with you.

He opened the door and stepped out into the night. It was quiet. Very quiet. The silence felt haunted as if he was not alone in it, as if there were hollowed-eyed ghosts watching him in the night. He shook the idea from his head. That was crazy thinking and if there was one thing Earl was not, it was crazy.

The school rose above him, dark and shadow-wreathed, a hulking mass of stone set with black windows. He inserted his key into the door of the service entrance and let himself in. Inside, the silence was worse. Every little sound he made was magnified, echoing down the empty corridors as if he were setting loose tiny ghosts with each movement.

No time for that.

He knew where he was going and he knew what he had to do. The Secret was quiet for a change. It had pushed him too far and now it was hiding in the shadows as things like it always did when you stood up to them.

He cut down E-section to the gym, then down another little corridor which was known as G. This was the place. He pushed through the door, staring down into the well of darkness before him. Red illumination glowed from an EXIT sign, but that was about it.

He turned on the light.

Better.

He took the stairway below. It led to the Girl's shower room. He moved down the steps and through the doorway with the EXIT sign poised above it. Inside, his boots clumped and echoed across the tile floor. He began to get excited because he could smell the dankness of the stalls, the pink soap and good, clean sweat of young, well-muscled bodies.

He passed the archway leading into the locker room and went directly into the shower room. He got an erection right away. Looking around, he went over to the clean air vent set high up on the wall near the ceiling. Using a screwdriver, he removed the grid and retrieved his Zetta Z12 Security Camcorder. He tucked it into his pocket and replaced the grid.

There.

Simple.

Now he had eight hours of feed to watch. He got hard again imagining all those hot little fucktwats parading around in the bare, their titties bouncing, water beaded on their thighs and taut rounded asses. He hoped that he got some good shots of his favorites—Summer Kierson, a tall, blue-eyed blonde; Jennifer Lake, a buxom redhead with a set on her that wouldn't quit; and of course Abby Salter. She was a petite little thing with spiky black hair and simmering dark eyes, beautiful long legs. God, those legs would crush you if you were in her saddle.

She's our favorite, the Secret said. *What a sweet little cup of sugar. I bet she tastes yummy. I bet if you sank your teeth into her hot little fucktwat it would taste like hot cherry fizz—*

The image of that was too much.

Earl stumbled back into the shower room, unzipping himself and masturbating there in one of the stalls, crying out in his passion. But it wasn't enough. His mind was filled with carnal images of the girls themselves, naked and dripping wet. He turned on the shower spigot, cold water spraying into his face and making him cry out, then hot water drenching him, filling the air with roiling steam as he moaned and came.

"AAAAWWWW!" he cried out.

Gasping, he leaned against the tile wall of the stall, his entire body shaking, clothes wringing wet, that gnawing sense of guilt and self-loathing slowly reinserting itself until he reached out and shut off the spigot.

Sobbing, he stepped out of the stall, pants around his knees, feeling filthy and degraded, shivering with excess and disgust at who and what he was.

He pulled himself together.

He had to get out of here.

If he was found like this…dear God, there would be no explaining it away. They would know. They would know exactly what he was.

Silly little perv, they probably already suspect.

He zipped his pants and stumbled from the shower room. As he passed the locker room, the desire began to kick up inside of him again. He thought of the girls dressing in there, sliding on all their delicate little underthings.

Might be something in the lockers, the Secret whispered inside his skull. *Something we can take with us, eh? Something left behind. Something we can touch and fondle and covet in private.*

Of course, his guilt would have no part of it even though the Secret urged him on, encouraging his self-degradation, gloating over his immoral lust and depravity.

He went into the locker room, turning on the light and that's when he saw all the clothes on the floor. It scared him…yet intrigued him. Heaps of gym shorts and t-shirts were cast about. All of them were stained a dirty black.

What the hell?

Then he remembered. The Middleburg Leopards girls' soccer team had had a game over in North Platte that night. They must have come back late.

But why would they throw their shorts and tees about? Rhonda Pheetan, their coach, was legendary for her OCD, raising hell with any of the girls that did not follow her exacting little instructions to the letter.

Earl didn't know Rhonda really. Enough to say hi, that was about it. Truth told, she generally sneered if he even looked in her direction.

Because she knows. She can smell it on you. Smell the dirt of your soul and the filth of your being, the perversion sweating foul from your pores, you vile little perv.

"Shut up," he said quietly, then with more volume: "SHUT UP!"

His voice boomed through the locker room, echoing down the rows of lockers and coming right back at him. When it quieted, leaving him standing there, a vague sort of fear bristling at his lower belly, he thought he heard a noise. A sort of rustling sound from the far end of the room.

Somebody's here, he thought then.

I'm not alone.

The idea of that was frightening. If someone was here that meant they had heard him in the shower room. There was no way they couldn't have. They might have even watched him.

They're hiding back there, the Secret told him. *You better go find them. You better shut them up so they can't tell.*

He knew what the Secret was hinting at, what he must do, but the idea was unthinkable. Yet, fear of discovery pushed him forward and he moved quietly down the nearest aisle of lockers to the area beyond them that led up to the gym itself.

He started seeing things right away that he did not like. There were filthy black handprints on the lockers, smears of dried blood and fleshy goo. On the floor, there were puddles of slime and coagulated blood, lots of gleaming little white things that looked very much like human teeth.

The smell in the air was horrible, like burnt grease, warm vomit, and the drainage of infected wounds.

As soon as he got there, he saw them.

The entire soccer team was there, some fourteen girls. They were just standing there, naked and unmoving like dime store dummies somebody had posed.

"You girls," Earl said in a weak voice. "What...what are you doing here?"

They did not answer.

And as he got closer and got a really good look at them in the dim lights, the heat that had been rising in his groin diminished. It went cold. He recognized some of the girls by name—Summer

Kierson and Brittany LaCree, Jenna Larsen and Holly VanderBeck—and others just by sight. All of them were white as sheets, their flesh perforated with holes the size of nickels and quarters. None of them had eyes and it did not look as if any of them had any teeth either, just puckering black holes that were opening and closing like the gills of fish.

"What is this about?" he said, knowing it had to be about something bad, real bad.

The girls just stood there.

Their mouths were moving so they weren't dead...but what had happened to them? He knew something like this needed to be called in, but how would he explain how he found them?

No, he couldn't risk getting involved.

Yet, he couldn't leave them.

He walked over to one of the nearest girls, Jenna Larsen, eyeing her up pretty good, studying her from her taut thighs to the line of blonde pubic hair to her flat belly and pointy little breasts.

He swallowed, the heat rising in his groin again.

The Secret giggled. *Only you could get turned on in this freakshow, Earl. Only you. Go ahead, indulge yourself. This little fucktwat can't see you. Finger her, feel the heat between her legs, all pink and soft melt-in-your-mouth yummy. Go ahead, touch her.*

By that point, Earl was breathing so hard he thought he was going to pass out. Cool water dripped from him and hot sweat joined it. His erection felt almost painful trapped in his pants.

Like dolls, Earl. Little honey-sweet fucktwat dolls for you to play with.

But he knew this was something he had to resist because it was all wrong and not in just the ethical sense, but wrong as in fucked-up and unnatural. His breath coming out hot between clenched teeth, eyes wide and staring in his head, he reached out to pinch Jenna's left nipple. Drool ran from his puffy lips and down his chin. He gripped her nipple between his thumb and first finger like the delicious little cherry blossom it was.

Her skin was abnormally hot. It practically burned to touch her...but he couldn't stop himself now. Despite the pain, he pinched her nipple with great force, clenching his teeth tighter and tighter...then it burst like a berry, spraying him with something that scalded his face. At the same time, a trickle of something like piss ran from between her legs, sizzling as it struck the floor.

But Earl didn't see that.

His face felt like it had been spattered with acid. But nipples didn't have acid in them—

The girls were all shivering now.

Except…it wasn't exactly shivering but a sort of slow undulation as if the muscles beneath their skin were rolling in peristaltic waves, rippling. He felt heat coming from them, an acrid, searing heat that rolled off them in sheets. The many holes in their bodies and faces were connecting now with minute cracks and jagged rents, steam rising, gathering in a heavy cloud over their heads. He saw a sort of blue electricity flickering inside them.

The lights dimmed.

Then went out.

Earl screamed because he had never liked the dark and he had always subconsciously feared the things that might live in it. The darkness was heavy, so thick it was almost furry. He heard the girls moving around him, the heat coming off them smothering him. He stumbled back and collided with one of the lockers and the reverberating noise drew them right to him.

Not in the dark, oh please not in the dark.

They were all around him and he was gasping for air, making a sort of croaking sound in his throat. A sizzling sound like bacon sputtering with hot grease came from them.

Then they touched him.

A dozen hands touched him, burning into his flesh and he screamed as their fingers seemed to coil over him like black, writhing worms. They were hot, blazing hot like knives heated over flames and they sliced right into him, his skin blackening and cracking open, his organs filling with bubbling hot gas and expanding like balloons, swelling him into a gurgling bag of skin. His eyes popped in steaming rivers of yellow pus and tissue about the same time his body exploded like a puffball, his insides erupting in a seething spray of blistering sap.

By then, he was quite dead and there were only the sounds of suckering mouths feeding on him.

When the lights flickered back into life some time later, the girls were gone, only the blackened progress of their footprints out of the locker room marking the fact that they had ever been there. On the floor, there was a set of burnt bones lying in the middle of a seeping, nauseous pool of congealed human tallow.

12

Be quiet, Abby told herself. *Be quiet like you've never been quiet before.*

She was crouched in the linen closet, two doors down from the room in which she had found Mrs. Pearson...or what she assumed was Mrs. Pearson. She held her hand over her mouth so she did not whimper or breathe too loudly, doing everything she could not to shake and make any noise.

The intruder was coming up the steps. It had paused at the top or, perhaps, just a few stairs shy of the landing. It was silent. She was silent. The waiting game had begun.

There's nobody up here, creep, so go away!

But it wouldn't be that easy and she knew it. What she had to do was control herself. Any little sound would alert what was out there to her location. Her face was wet with tears, her stomach tight as a clenched fist. She mastered her breathing so it was barely a whisper. Nobody out there would be able to hear it.

God, if she only had her iPhone! She'd left it on the table over at the Sumners. Great thinking.

The stairs creaked and she knew that whoever it was was now upstairs with her. She heard a hollow clump of heavy boots on the landing. And...breathing. Something like breathing. A hollow sound of respiration like air blown down a pipe. A hissing, rushing sort of noise.

Now the boots—if boots they were—were coming up the hallway. *Clump, clump, clump.* They paused just down the corridor, in front of the bathroom. Now they were moving again, making straight down the hall past the linen closet for the bedroom with the remains. The intruder went in there and, apparently, just stood there a time, perhaps studying the wreck of Mrs. Pearson in some detail.

In the dark?

Abby didn't know. The only thing she was truly certain of by that point, other than her fear, was that whoever or *whatever* this was, they were probably responsible for what had happened. She didn't know this for a fact, but the feeling she had was resolute.

Clump, clump, clump.

They boots were coming back. They had paused down there as if whoever wore them was casting for scent like a bloodhound. She was sweating profusely now. There was a cry in her throat she had to choke down. She could not make a sound. Dear God, she had to be totally quiet because…because whatever was out there was *listening* for her. She was sure of it.

The boots were coming again, moving in closer.

Clump, clump, clump.

They were paused right outside the door now. Only a few inches of hardwood separated her from the horror that had come out of the night. She could hear it breathing with that sibilant sound that made chills swarm up her spine. Its smell, so close like this, was acrid and burning…like the stink of battery acid. The air in the closet actually began to feel hot. Then, coming from under the door she saw flickering light and heard a sort of sizzling sound.

Then the boots clomped off down the hallway and she heard them going down the stairs.

This wasn't right—that smell, that flickering glow, and what had happened to Mrs. Pearson—none of it was right. Wiping sweat from her face, she was certain that what had gotten to Mrs. Pearson and what had been standing outside the door could not possibly be human.

She waited.

She needed to get back to Megan. That was a priority, but it wouldn't do any good to get killed in the process. But Mrs. Pearson…Jesus, what had that thing done to her?

She was burnt to ash but she still was able to speak.

How was that possible?

How was any of this possible?

There were too many questions and uncertainties in her brain and she couldn't sort them out hiding here in the dark. Carefully, she opened the door and stepped out into the darkness. Everything was quiet. She took a few steps towards the stairs and then paused, listening.

She heard nothing.

Had that thing left the house now?

Maybe it did. Maybe it's next door now. Maybe it's at the Sumners. Maybe it's searching around for something living over there and if Megan cries, it will know right where to go.

Abby suppressed her panic.

She had to use her head. She had to get out of here, but she had to do it in a safe, practical sort of way. Megan was counting on her. Who knew when Mr. and Mrs. Sumner would be home?

Her night vision wasn't good, but good enough that she could see the stairs. The bathroom door was open. She went in there. If her sense of orientation was correct, then the window would give her a good view of the Sumner house next door.

She stepped in there.

She could see the Sumner's side yard and the sidewalk out front. She saw a shape moving, sort of shambling down the walk. It didn't look right at all, too much like that creeping shadow she'd seen coming up the stairwell.

She gasped.

Now and again there was a discharge of cool blue light from the shape as if some sort of electrical energy were leaking from it. Then it was hidden by the hedges out front. Across King Street, she saw two more dim forms with that same weird shine to them.

It brought a terror and a paranoia that was inescapable. What if something had happened out there, something really terrible and the whole goddamn town was filled with things like that? The image that thought created in her mind was of walking dead things, nightmare zombies charged with some deadly energy seeking out the last living souls of Middleburg.

Oh, that was crazy, it was insane, it was—

Abby didn't care what it was. Inside, she believed it and believing it, knew she was in incredible danger.

Megan.

Dangerous or not, she could not afford to waste any more time. She would go get the baby and then…and then…well, she didn't know, but they were getting the hell out of that house to somewhere safe until she could figure out just what in the heck was going on. Her mom. Yes, her mom would know what to do. Her mom *always* knew what to do.

It was a plan.

She left the bathroom, pausing again momentarily outside the door. She listened. She heard nothing but the rush of wind in the treetops outside. It sounded safe. She started down the steps. On the third step, she froze up. She didn't know why, but it was like an icy fear exploded inside her and she simply froze up. *Oh no, oh no.* She remembered that the flashlight was still in her hand.

She clicked it on.

Just before the beam came on, she saw a strobing phosphorescence. Then the light was on, illuminating the entire stairwell and particularly the hulking shape waiting at the bottom of the steps. It was dark and twisted, a grotesque manlike shape with reaching hands that were gnarled and skeletal, the flesh scarred and torn open, hanging in loops like the cerements of a mummy. Right before the beam was cancelled out, she saw a grim, distorted visage like a mask of bone, the flesh pocked and pitted with irregular fissures.

And it had no eyes, just empty steaming holes punched into its face.

That's Jim Jensen, a thought telegraphed through her mind. The long black hair and thick, shaggy black beard surrounding that pallid face could only be Jim Jensen who mowed lawns, did landscaping, and odd jobs throughout the summer. His appearance had always been intimidating like some Manson cultist, but he was a decent, friendly guy, always on his cell, always texting his friends.

But not anymore.

Something had changed.

Something had transformed him into a monster.

Abby let out a cry and threw the dead flashlight at him, climbing back up the steps. Panicking in the darkness, she ran right into the wall, feeling her way down its length until she reached the door to the bedroom with the remains of Mrs. Pearson.

She saw that flickering light coming on.

The thing was coming for her.

She locked the door, trying to think and not scream. The window. It was the only way. She dashed for it and ran into the rocking chair, flipping it and Mrs. Pearson over. A cloud of spinning ash filled the feeble rays of moonlight shining through the pane.

Abby tore the curtains free and tossed them aside.

She heard the fist of the thing pounding at the door. That eerie blue-white light flickered under it like the luminous tongues of snakes. She slid the window up and kicked out the screen.

As the door burst open with an explosion of light and force, she climbed out the window and...fell. She hit the porch roof, sliding down it and hanging on by her fingertips. She dropped into the hedges, scratching her face and hands. She rolled into the wet grass and then was on her feet, running for the Sumner house.

I'm coming, baby. I'm coming.

13

"What kind of shit town is this?" Clarice Stebbens said as she piloted her lacquer-black Infinity QX down the empty streets of Middleburg.

She'd been in town less than five minutes but that was more than enough to form an opinion. At least, in her book it was. She was only passing through to fuel up, then she was going to ditch this shit stain and get back out onto the interstate to civilization. She watched all the dark houses flash by and was amazed that people could live—and be happy—in such comparative squalor. A born and bred city girl, Clarice did not find small towns pretty as a postcard or quaint, but downright creepy.

"Turn left at the next corner," the Navigator told her.

She slowed considerably, realizing she was doing nearly fifty miles an hour down the quiet streets of Shitburg—as she was beginning to think of it—which were clearly posted at thirty. She had to calm down. She was wound pretty tight right about then, but a lot was on the line and she needed to get home as fast as possible. All she wanted was a quick gas-up and then back to the interstate. Getting pulled over by the locals for speeding or clipping some pedestrian certainly would not help matters.

Just mellow out already, take it slow.

But that wasn't quite so easy. She had to get home and smooth things over with Mathew. Oh, he suspected all right, she knew as she hung the left onto another equally dismal, deserted street. There had been too many late nights, too many suppers missed. She could only blame so much of it on the high pressure world of mega-dollar real estate. When she broke it off with Derek that night after a tumble at the Sleepy Hollow hotel, he had been incensed. He ranted and raved.

She tried to calm him. "Listen, I'm a married woman. We had our fun but you knew going into this it couldn't last forever."

"So you're dumping me cold?"

"Hardly cold," she said, considering the fact that his semen was still drying on her thighs. "It had to come to a stop and now it has. This can only end in disaster, so we need to stop it before it does. We need to...prioritize."

That's when he really went livid and turned about three shades of purple. She was afraid. Really afraid. She thought he was going to kill her. But Derek wasn't that type. He calmed down after a good bout of swearing. Then, almost casually, he got dressed.

"I guess I can understand your position, Claire. I mean, let's face it, you're married to a very rich man and you stand to lose a great deal."

"I'm glad you're being reasonable."

Derek smiled thinly. "Yes, I'm being adult. And as an adult, I believe in full disclosure. That's why I'm leaving now and when I get home, I'm going to call your husband and tell him how I've been fucking you."

With that, he stepped out the door.

For a moment or two, Claire had been stunned, then she panicked. She jumped out of bed and went after him, only realizing as she got outside and her bare feet slapped on the pavement that she was naked. She dashed back inside, dressed, and by the time she got back out there, Derek was gone.

And she was about to step into the deepest shit of her life.

She had to get home and salvage things. There was always the possibility that Derek had been bluffing. But if he had indeed made the call, then things were going to get ugly. If Mathew knew, he would be waiting for her. He would pour them both a brandy and sit her down. Then he would say something like, *I'm not going to beat you up like some wronged husband, Claire. I'm not even going to slap you across the face like the cheap little slut you are. I'm only going to ask you why. I've given you pretty much everything, so it makes no sense to me that you'd betray me. So tell me why. That's all I ask.* Then like the high-priced trial lawyer he indeed was, he'd sit down. *You can begin talking at any time.* And that would be the worst part of it—his composure. He would be like ice that no flame could ever thaw.

And what would she say?

She had been bored? She had been horny? She wanted some excitement in her life? She had made a tactical error? Maybe it was all those things coupled with a hereditary weakness for bad choices and an almost inbred lack of self-discipline. Because, realistically, nearly all married women have the chance to fool around they just know better.

But she didn't know better.

If he divorces me on the grounds of adultery, I'll come away with nothing but a minor stipend. I'll be out on the rocks, I'll be broke, I'll be ruined.

No, no, no. She had to make this right.

Jesus, where was that fucking gas station?

"Half a mile on the right," the Navigator said.

"Shut the fuck up," she told it.

She still had a good hour's drive until she got home. God knows what damage Derek would bring about in that span of time. Nervous, trembling, she plucked her Galaxy S5 from her bag and keyed her home number. It rang and rang. Did Mathew already know? If that was the case, he might not even bother answering. He would know she was coming, hot from her adulterer's bed, loins still steamy with man-dew, and he would let her stew in the foul juices of her own infidelity and treachery.

The phone was answered. "Where are you?" Mathew wanted to know.

"I'm on my way right now. Be there in an hour."

"Will you?"

"Yes. It all went later than I thought but I think we have the whole Citibank thing nailed now. I'll tell you about it when I get there."

"I can't wait to hear."

There was sarcasm under his words but then there was always sarcasm with him as if what she did was minor in comparison to his legendary exploits in the courtroom.

"Yes, I'll...Mathew? Mathew?"

The Galaxy dropped the call.

Shit! Fuck! Shit!

Of all times. She tried to reconnect and got only static. Good God, of all times. So much was riding on this. She was tempted to toss the phone out the window but she knew she couldn't blame the Galaxy; it was this stupid little town, Shitburg, stuck in the middle of nowhere. That was the real problem. She watched the houses roll by and she couldn't make up her mind if they reminded her more of outhouses lined up in rows or gravestones. Goddamn worthless little shit nugget of a town—

Jesus!

There was a girl standing right in the middle of the road! Claire swung the wheel at the last possible moment and saw the parked car right in front of her Infinity. She hit it and hit it hard with a jarring impact and a screech of metal. Then the wheel spun from her hands and the SUV popped the curb and slammed right into what had to be the mother of all elm trees.

She lost consciousness for a moment or two and when came out of it, she was nearly hysterical. She cried out and fought against the safety belt…then she relaxed, realizing that she was not injured, save for a sore shoulder and abdomen from the belt crushing her in an anaconda-like embrace.

The Infinity was dead.

Even the dash lights were out. Nothing. Kaput. She unbuckled her belt and gasped for breath. The police would be coming. God only knew when she'd get home now. Another complication. She plucked her cell off the seat and stepped out into the night.

It was black out there, the wind felt dry and gritty. As her eyes adjusted, she realized it wasn't as dark as she had originally thought though a streetlight across the way was definitely out.

That girl.

Yes, where was that fucking girl and what was she doing out in the middle of the street in the first place? Claire leaned against the dead hulk of the Infinity, getting angry because she didn't have time for this shit. Of all nights, this was positively the very worst.

She tried her Galaxy again.

Nothing.

The display flickered and went out and that didn't make a lick of sense because she knew damn well it was charged. She always kept it charged.

Where were the fucking police?

She should have heard a siren by now, something. But what she found even stranger was the fact that nobody had come out to find out what was going on. The houses behind her and across the street were still black. Surely, someone had heard the crash. It was inconceivable that they hadn't.

Claire stepped out into the middle of the street.

She could not see a light on in a single house. What was it? A blackout? A power failure? There should have been a light somewhere. The moon was shining down, breaking through clumps of leaden clouds, but that was about it.

She heard a crackling sound behind her.

At first, it reminded her of someone balling up a cigarette pack cellophane in their fist...but it was more like static electricity, she realized. She turned and saw no one.

The crackling was off to her left now.

The moonlight punched through the clouds and she saw the girl standing there. She was no more than twelve or thirteen, blonde braids falling over shoulders. She wore a white nightgown that was smeared with filth. *Who would let her go out like that?* A stink came off her, a hot smell of scorched meat that reminded Claire of the burn ward that her brother had died in.

"What the hell were you doing out in the middle of the road?" Claire demanded of her.

In the moonlight, the girl did not answer. Her head was cocked to the side like that of a confused puppy...or a man who'd been hanged. She was about fifteen feet away at that point and Claire knew there was something very wrong about her that went far beyond her filthy nightgown or that burning stink that wafted from her.

"Why don't you answer me?" she said, her words sounding fragile as she began to grow first nervous, then very afraid.

The girl just stood there, shadows deepening around her. Eddies of blue light danced over her body. One of them sparked in her hair and a puff of smoke rose from it. Then it seemed like every part of her was suddenly moving—the nightgown was billowing, her braids flying out in wild loops as if they were caught in a strong wind, her entire body jerking with contorted, whiplashing movements as if she were undergoing a series of devastating seizures...or was charged with high voltage.

She came closer and Claire stepped back. Her hammering heart felt like it had dropped in a cold mass just south of her stomach. She was terrified and helpless, reality tearing open right in front of her, her guts feeling as if they'd pulled themselves inside out. She stumbled backwards, nearly tripping over the curb, until she felt the solid, reassuring mass of the Infinity.

And the girl came forward, jerking and twitching like she was being electrocuted, something about her gaining intensity and power and triumphant evil. She held out hands to Claire that were sizzling and sputtering, plumes of smoke rising from them, the fingertips blazing with cold blue flames like the candlewicks of a hand of glory.

Claire screamed.

And as she did so, the girl mocked her with a screeching wail that took the wind right out of her. An oily stink of fear exuded from her pores as the thing—and it *was* a thing—moved towards her with outstretched fingers arcing with cold blue tongues of energy, a twisted, shriveled wraith from a grave.

The girl's face was like white rubber that had been sheared open in too many places, one gash reaching from the corner of her mouth up to her left cheekbone. Fingers of smoke issued from the wounds. In fact, it issued from her fingertips and the black suckering hole of her mouth and even from the eye sockets themselves that were empty pockets of red pared flesh. Her entire body was smoldering like a burning witch, lit from the inside like some luminous paper lantern.

When she was five feet away and Claire could feel the pulsating waves of heat coming from her, the girl screamed like a dozen moaning ghosts.

And Claire bolted.

She ran right at the horror, then cut to the right, nearly making it. But the girls fingertips brushed her upper arm and it felt like she had been kicked. She was knocked four feet, skidding over the pavement, her arm filled with pins and needles, her shoulder feeling like it was twisted around in its socket.

But she kept moving, survival instinct pushing her forward, making her crawl over the road until she found her feet and started to run. Her arm hanging dead and limp at her side, her leather blazer burnt, her head full of shrill screaming noise, she ran and kept running, not daring to look behind her.

14

Joe Sumner turned as the voice spoke to him, a sharp stab of icy fear cutting through him. He wheeled around and saw a woman standing there with a white apron on. There was a bloody smear down it as if she had vomited blood and maybe she had at that because her chin was glistening red as were her lips. She had a mop of frizzy red hair that was stained with oily black streaks like some bad dye job. There was a cold sore on her lower lip that looked unpleasantly juicy like a berry.

"What...what did you say?" he asked.

"I said, you should've gotten out while you still could," she replied, her voice dry and scratching. "It's too late now...the rain came down...the black rain. I went out to my car...I had to see if the windows were rolled up...then it came down."

"Oh," Joe said, knowing how absolutely ridiculous that sounded but simply muttering the first thing that came to mind.

"The black rain," she growled. "It burned...it burned my face and my eyes. It was like hot needles piercing me. God, it hurt...it hurt so bad...then like hail falling. Burning hail."

Hot black rain? Burning hail? What the hell was she talking about?

Maybe she was crazy. She certainly looked the part. Her face had a strained, corded look to it, the skin waxy and yellow as if she were jaundiced. When she spoke, he could see that her teeth were bad, gnarled and uneven, stained pink. But the worst thing was her left eye which was a bright succulent red like a Maraschino cherry. Tears of blood ran from it. The pupil—tiny and black like a bead—stared off towards the window as if the muscle had been sheared.

"I'll get you some help," he said.

She giggled, mouth opening wide and giving him a view of those awful teeth jutting from gums that were speckled black. They looked like headstones rising from black cemetery earth. As she laughed, one of them fell out and she spit it to the floor.

The cell phone dropped from his fingers.

"They're all falling out," she told him.

As if to prove it, she gripped one of her upper central incisors with thumb and forefinger and yanked it out effortlessly, setting it on the counter. It was gray, infected looking, a few droplets of blood glistening on the countertop.

"No way out now. Those that were in the rain and hail...they're everywhere." She laughed with a mordant cackling that reminded him of a cartoon witch. *"We're* everywhere now."

Joe had no idea what she had but it was bad, real bad. She coughed out a fine mist of blood and he drew back as if it might be contaminated with something. She wiped her hands on her apron and they left greasy gray streaks. Her entire body was convulsing like maybe there was something inside her that wanted to come out.

"You need a doctor."

"Too late now."

And, yes, he believed that it was. She reached in his direction and he involuntarily backed up. She let out a shrill, animal-like cry and three more teeth fell out. She spit them to the floor with a slime of blood. *"Sick,"* she said. "Real...*sick."*

Sick as in contagion, he decided. As in plague and pestilence. If what she said was true about the black rain and hail, then whatever had been in it must have done this to her. She continued to quake and shake like her nerves were malfunctioning. Now and again, she'd jerk stiff as a board and let out a little cry. She was blocking the way out from behind the counter. He was going to have to swing himself right over the top. There was no way in hell he was going to let her get any closer.

His heart was beating with a wild, frantic rhythm of the sort he hadn't known since high school when he ran track.

He moved back a few steps as she came a few inches closer. Then she threw back her head and her mouth yawned open, an awful strident scream coming out. And as she did so, he saw that the hand she was reaching towards him with had gone positively white. It was almost transparent, more like jelly than flesh. The vein networking stood out lividly.

And then she began to crack open.

That's what it looked like. She began to crack like glass. The back of her hand split open with three or four jagged rents, but no blood came out, just a thin watery discharge. More teeth dropped from her mouth with a tangle of blood. Mucus that was a purple-black in color ran from her left nostril. Her face began to split open, too, with ragged holes. Her left, bulging red eye collapsed into a river of red slime that dripped down her cheek. The right was sucked back into its socket with a juicy sound.

He couldn't help himself; he screamed.

It came out of him completely unbidden. He stumbled back, overturning a rack of Cheetos. She was moving towards him, a sputtering sound coming from inside her. Fingers of steam issued from her eye sockets and the holes in her face. It came from her fingertips and even her hair, making it look like it was smoldering.

She opened her puckering toothless maw and made a sort of low hissing noise.

The lights began to flicker.

Then Joe fled.

He ran straight towards the back, leapfrogging the skeleton and its attendant flesh pool and smashing into racks of hot dog and hamburger buns. There was a door and he pulled it open, falling out into the empty parking lot.

Behind him, the smoldering woman made a moaning, unearthly sound like a banshee.

15

As Charlie Shaw made his way back to King Street, he became aware of a strong, scorched odor in the streets. It smelled like there was a good fire going somewhere and maybe more than one. There even seemed to be a haze in the air. It was the sort of small town odor you smelled on January nights when fireplaces and wood stoves were going full-tilt.

He didn't like any of it.

He kept thinking of those people, those smoldering people. He didn't know what that was about but it scared him bad. He didn't like the idea of Candy being home alone with—*well, go on and say it then*—monsters roaming wild in the streets. No, it all bothered him in the worst way and made him leg it that much faster over to King where he planned on packing up Candy, jumping in her Taurus, and getting the fuck out of Dodge.

When we're somewhere safe, he thought, *some motel on down the road, then I'll call the State Patrol. I won't waste my time with the townies.*

He wished to God he had one of those damn cell phones right then and there. He wanted badly to call Candy and get her moving. He supposed he could have detoured to some all-night greasy spoon or gas station and gave her a jingle, but that, like knocking on somebody's front door and begging to use the phone, took time.

And the way he was seeing things, he just didn't have any goddamn time to waste.

Again, he felt a certain heartache for the 1970s when there were actual phone booths in Middleburg. There used to be five or six of them in town.

The closer he got to King, the more crazy ideas started occurring to him. Crap culled from late night horror movies and TV shows he'd seen as a kid. What if everyone was like those things? What if the whole dang town was overrun with them? And what if he couldn't get out?

But that was nonsense.

Sheer nonsense.

Still, there was no getting around the fact that those people somehow had a very strange effect on the electrical system of his Chevy. He didn't know what that was about anymore than he knew what any of this was about.

He kept going because it wasn't far now.

He would be there in twenty minutes or less which didn't seem like long, but Charlie knew each one of them would be like a nail pounded into him as he worried about his wife.

Funny, he got to thinking, *how it takes something like this to show you where your priorities lie.*

And that was the truth. He was like most married men in that he didn't spend a great deal of time thinking about his spouse. Candy was Candy and she had always been there, it seemed, and she always would be. He took her for granted same way she took him for granted, he supposed, and that was the way of relationships whose heat cooled with the passing years. But now, feeling that it was all hanging in some precarious balance, he was worried that something terrible was going to happen to her. And, worse, that something already had.

Wait.

Over there.

The house in the middle of the block. That was Rick Pacek's house. Looked like the lights were on. Charlie and Rick had bowled together for years. He'd just stop in quick and use his phone. Rick wouldn't mind at all. He was an old bachelor, retired from the railroad, and had had very little going on.

Charlie jogged over there.

He rang the doorbell a few times, then knocked very loudly. There was no answer. Not so much as a shuffle of footsteps from inside. Shit. He tried the doorbell again. *C'mon, Rick!* But there was nothing. Out of desperation, Charlie tried the screen door. It was open. The other door wasn't even closed tightly. He pushed it wide and stepped inside.

"Hey, Rick!" he called. "Hey, Rick! It's me, Charlie Shaw. Need to use your phone real quick."

The silence was unbroken.

It didn't mean anything necessarily. Rick was getting on in years. Maybe he had fallen asleep in front of the TV or he was upstairs dropping a deuce. These were the things that ran through Charlie's head, but none of them gained any traction.

His heart began to beat a bit faster.

He didn't know what it was exactly, but he began to get a real bad feeling. He stepped into the living room and nothing was out of place. Everything seemed fine. But there was a smell in the air that reminded him of those damn monsters. A hot, burnt sort of stink. He went from the living room into the kitchen, turning on the light. There was the phone. He helped himself to it, feeling very nervous when he turned his back to the living room as if something might suddenly jump out at him.

The phone was dead.

There was sort of a distant buzzing on the line, but nothing more. He punched in his home phone number. Nothing. He tried 911. Nothing. Shit. He hung it up and went back into the living room as that sense of unease threading through him began to enlarge, began to fill him. His breathing was labored now and a fine dew of sweat had broken out on his face.

Something's bad here and you better get your ass out of here before you find out what.

Yes, not only that but he needed to get to Candy. Still, Rick was an old friend. He just couldn't turn his back on him. That wasn't right and it sure as hell was not ethical in the broader sense. Rick wouldn't have left until he was sure Charlie was okay. That's the kind of guy he was. Very straight-up, very honest, very old school.

Okay.

Charlie clicked on the hall light. Right away he saw something he did not like. There were dirty footprints leading off down the carpeted hallway and that burnt smell was not just stronger, it was positively gagging. He tried to tell himself that it probably meant nothing, but he was certain it meant everything.

Those footprints…

He crouched down and looked closer. They weren't stained as from dirty boots, they were burned right into the nap of the carpet itself right down to the backing beneath. That would have taken a lot of heat. He followed them down the hallway for a few feet.

There was something caught in each of them that glittered like silica or metallic dust.

Funny.

He reached down to touch it, then pulled his hand away. No, there was something wrong about this and the last thing he wanted to do was to come in contact with it...whatever it was.

He followed the prints to the end of the hallway with his eyes. He saw that there was a door at the very end and there were two smeared black handprints on it.

You goddamn well know what that means.

And he did. Oh, but he certainly did. He'd seen what those things did to the paint of his pickup just by placing their hands on it. Whatever had come into this house was one of them and he wasn't about to play hero and try to hunt them down.

Feeling a fear down deep in his belly, Charlie turned and headed for the front door. He didn't start breathing easier until he was off the porch and his lungs were filled with the damp air of the night.

He was about twenty feet down the sidewalk when he saw the lights in Rick's house begin to flicker and then go out completely.

Then he started to run again.

16

Tommy McCleesh pulled his cab up to the curb outside Barred & Bottled and tapped his fingers on the steering wheel as he waited for old Bill to come out. Same thing every Saturday night: one a.m. and Bill needed a lift. He'd be half in the bag and full of stories as he was every night. Bill didn't bother to call for a ride because Tommy was always there waiting for him. He'd help him into the cab, take a swing around the park while Bill talked about the old days and then he'd take him home, get him into the house and his favorite recliner so he didn't fall and hurt himself.

This had been going on for nearly four years by that point so there was no reason tonight would be any different.

Tommy went on at midnight and when he got to the cabstand, Jerome was the only one there. *No one else showed,* he said. *Funny night, real funny night.* And Tommy had to agree with him there. Maybe it was the storm, but the streets were dead. A little rain usually didn't stop the faithful, but tonight was different somehow.

The wind blew debris and cycling clouds of dust up the empty walks. There was something creepy about that.

Like it never rained at all, Tommy thought. *So dry out there.*

He checked his watch. "Come on, Billy boy. You're late."

Give him another five minutes, then you better go get him.

There was no rush. No traffic tonight, no activity, hardly any calls at all according to Jerome. Radio had been acting strange, lots of interference. He tried it and got nothing but static. A lot of the drivers were using cells now, but Tommy didn't believe in them and he refused to be part of the problem.

Eventually, he supposed, he'd have to break down and get one.

Like fuck I will.

Sitting there, he fired up a cigarette. He knew Bill wouldn't mind. He looked down the street. The houses and buildings looked drab and gray as if the rain had washed the color out of them. The only thing to break it up was the blinking yellow light down at the end of Hurley where it crossed Four Points. Blink on, blink off. All night like that.

He finished his cigarette and watched someone across the street moving down the walk. They—it was hard to say if they were male or female—moved with a strange shuffling sort of gait. Some weirdo apparently. They crossed the street and passed by the front of the bar and—

What the hell?

As they moved past the car, he saw what appeared to be flickering fingers of blue light emitted from them. He just sat there, frozen in silence. The lights on the cab dimmed, the dashboard display following suit. The cab stalled.

By the time he looked up, they were gone.

He killed the headlights and turned the cab over. The engine barely caught. What the heck was going on? He needed to get this rig back to the garage before it died completely.

Shit.

He got out and went into the bar. He didn't have all night to wait for Bill. He pushed through the door and was greeted by a heavy, abnormal silence and a stench that nearly put him to his knees. Christ, it was foul, just absolutely rank. He acquainted it with singed hair and burnt grease, a hot, meaty smell.

But if the stink was bad, what he saw made it seem positively pedestrian. It made him fall back against the door, the breath caught in his throat. He could feel his blood pressure spike dramatically, his face prickly-hot from it. His temples throbbed with every manic beat of his heart. Fear was like a cold brick in his chest. He was incapacitated momentarily. He could not even blink. His eyes felt too big for their sockets.

You're not seeing this shit. There's no way in hell you're seeing any of this.

That's what the voice of reason was telling him. He finally managed to blink his eyes. He saw the bottles of booze lined up behind the bar, the neon PABST sign in the window, the Tombstone pizza advert tacked to the wall between a couple of kitschy/funny placards: BOOZE IS THE ANSWER...ANYBODY REMEMBER WHAT THE QUESTION WAS? and I DON'T HAVE A DRINKING PROBLEM. I DRINK. I GET DRUNK. I

FALL DOWN. NO PROBLEM. If some music had been coming from the juke, it might have seemed like any other night at Barred & Bottled.

But it wasn't any other night.

Because on any other night there were not skeletons slumped in the booths. For one dizzy moment, Tommy even thought it might be a gag. But this was no gag. This was deadly serious.

He stepped over to the nearest booth and saw that the two skeletons were still steaming. The stink of that was sickening. They were still articulated, skulls thrown back, jaws agape. Strings of goo like cooled tallow were hanging from them, tangled in their rib slats and oozing from their skulls. The stuff had puddled on the tables, dripping to the floor in ribbons.

Bits of blackened material clung to them that must have been the remains of their clothes. Whatever did this, it must have taken incredible heat or cremating energy.

At the next booth, there was another skeleton with its skull facedown on the table as if it had drunk too much. One skeletal hand still clutched a mug half filled with beer, more of that pink, bubbling goo slopped over the table and hanging from the bones in glistening threads. It looked like a pool of gummy wax of the floor.

Absently, Tommy stepped in it and let out a choked cry as his shoe skidded across its oily surface. He pulled his foot back and filaments of the goo were stuck to the bottom of his shoe like strings of melted cheese.

He thought: *It must have happened fast, real fast. So fast that nobody even bothered trying to get away from it.*

He stumbled away, over to the bar. The antique St. Pauly Girl mirror hanging above the bottles was discolored with black streaks as if exposed to a blast of searing heat. On the bar top, he saw several blackened handprints burned into the wood. One of them looked like it had belonged to a child. Behind the bar, there was a collection of bones burnished brown that he did not bother studying.

This was madness.

This was insanity.

This was beyond anything his mind could wrap itself around.

Feeling like his knees were made of rubber, Tommy made it over to the door and pulled it open. Behind him, he heard a clattering as one of the skeletons tipped over and hit the floor like thrown dice.

That was enough.

He got out into the fresh air, his stomach convulsing almost painfully. Leaning against the hood of the cab, he tried to keep it down but it all came gushing out of him. He vomited into the street until it was all out of him, everything he'd eaten in the past twelve hours.

He leaned there, panting.

Get moving. Whatever happened to them can happen to you. You better believe that.

As he climbed into the cab, it was all swirling around and around in his head: that awful stink in there, the bones browned as if they'd been scorched, the handprints and that mist of steam in the air. He began to tie it together with that weirdo he'd seen that seemed to have light coming from them.

What did it mean?

What could it possibly mean?

He sipped from his coffee and lit another cigarette. He tried the radio but it still wasn't working right. Okay. No matter. He was going to drive over to the cop shop and report this and then he was going home and he was going to lock his fucking door.

Something had literally gone to hell in this town and he honestly did not want to know what it was.

17

Abby entered the Sumner house wired with her own terror. She stalked like a cat, listening, waiting, knowing she had to get to baby Megan but also knowing she had to get to her alive.

The thing that stopped her as she stepped into the kitchen was that same awful smell. It wasn't as bad here, just a suggestion of it compared to what it had been like at Mrs. Pearson's house.

But it was still there.

Pungent.

Pervasive.

She stepped through the kitchen in the darkness. She tried the lights by the door and there was nothing. She knew a few things about those monsters in the night and one of them was that they seemed to drain electrical energy. She'd seen it happen when Jim Jensen came up the stairs and when she'd put the flashlight beam on him when he was at the bottom—the house lights had dimmed and went off and the flashlight did the same. Being in the dark with them was suicidal, but if you had lights on and they went out, then you'd know.

It was something.

The fuse box.

That's it. You've seen dad do it. There's nothing to it...but where is it?

She tried to think. Where in the hell was the fusebox? She'd seen it earlier. She just had to think. Something which was not so easy with her present state of mind. Had she seen it in the basement when she'd gone down there to fetch the frozen pizza for supper? No, no, she didn't think so.

Got it.

It was in the pantry. Maybe there wasn't one of those things in the house and maybe throwing the breaker wouldn't bring the lights back, but it was worth a try. She crossed the kitchen carefully, feeling her heartbeat in her throat, knowing that any moment one of those...*people* might show. Easy does it. The moonlight coming in through the window guided her towards the back where the pantry door was. Her fingers found the knob.

She opened it.

Nothing jumped out at her.

She found the fuse box easily and opened the little door on it. She was going strictly by feel now. *Find the main. It's the big switch.* There. She had it. She flipped it and the lights thankfully came back on. Whatever those things were and whatever kind of energy they put out—or took away for that matter—it had tripped the breaker.

Good.

She went back out into the kitchen. She heard voices speaking from the living room. The Sumners? *It's the TV, dorkwad.* Yes, that's all it was. Crestfallen, she went into the living room and it was definitely the TV. She rather doubted the Sumners would be in there chatting about the incredible Veggetti—*Turn vegetables into healthy spaghetti!*—which was available for $14.95—*but wait! There's more! If you're one of the first 200 callers, you get a free Hot Potato Pocket.* She shut the TV off.

She grabbed the baby monitor and listened.

It was quiet upstairs.

Was that good or bad?

On the floor she found her iPhone...it was melted into an unrecognizable mass of plastic. So melted, in fact, that it was stuck to the hardwood floor. What the hell was that about? They couldn't get her so they got her phone? What sense was there to that?

Abby decided it wasn't worth thinking about.

By that point, she'd been in the house less than two minutes and each second was an eternity as she made her way to the stairs, climbing them slowly but wanting to run up them. But that wasn't smart and she knew it.

She clicked on the light at the top of the stairs and sighed when there was no one in the hallway. Okay. Now to Megan's room. This was the part that filled her with exhilaration...and terror. Exhilaration because she knew she had to get to the baby ASAP. And terror because she was afraid of what she might find.

She opened the door, something inside her cringing because it expected to be greeted by a nauseating burnt smell...but that wasn't the case. The room had a good, clean, sweet baby smell to it.

Abby turned on the nightlight, which was in the form of a carrot and went over to the crib.

Megan was gone.

No, no, no, she can't be! She can't be!

And she wasn't. She had merely scooted herself up into the corner against the bumper pad. Abby felt an enormous amount of tension run out of her. Megan was fine. So what now? One of them had been here (her phone was evidence of that) but they had not gone after the baby.

Because Megan was sleeping quietly. That thing couldn't find you either when you hid in the closet and that's because it didn't have eyes. None of them probably have eyes. They seek sounds.

Did that explain her smart phone?

No, but it was a start.

First things first. She went out into the hallway and called home on the landline. Nothing but a weird, shrilling sort of static. Hmm. She even tried 911 and Mrs. Sumner's cell. Nothing and nothing.

You're on your own here.

Okay, then.

There was only one reasonable thing to do as far as she was concerned and that was to pack up baby Megan and leg it over to her house. Mom would know what to do. It was only four blocks. That wasn't too far. Megan was a good baby and she wouldn't mind the jaunt. Great kid. Woke up happy and went to sleep happy.

First, Abby packed up the diaper bag with everything she would need including extra Onesies, sleepers, and blankets, making sure she grabbed Meggy's Nuk. Didn't dare go anywhere without that. Once she was satisfied, she gently woke Megan by stroking her back and whispering to her.

Megan came out of it with a lot of lip smacking and cooing sounds. Her dark hair stuck up in spikes, matching the color of her eyes. "Bumgoogum?" she said.

"That's right, Megs. Time for a midnight frolic."

Abby put the bag, a Gerber backpack type, around her shoulders and gathered up Megan, scooping her blanket around her. In her mint sleep suit, she would be plenty warm. They went downstairs, Megan blinking at the intrusion of light and Abby quickly scrawled a message on the dry erase board. *WE WENT TO MY HOUSE.* It wouldn't be the first time Megan had slept over so the Sumners wouldn't mind, particularly when they learned the details.

Last but not least, she took a bottle from the fridge and tucked into the battery-operated bottle warming pouch. If Megan needed it, it would be ready.

Abby turned off the lights and stepped out onto the porch with the baby. King Street looked empty. It was now or never.

"Ubbagubba," Megan said distastefully as the warm wind brushed her pink, plump face.

"Tell me about it," Abby said.

18

All right, Mr. fucking Tiddles, where did you get off to now?

Melody Marris stood on the back porch in her scarlet robe, her hair pulled back in a ponytail, her eyes barely open and a Kleenex pressed to her red, irritated nose.

"Come on, puppy dog," she said, coughing and clearing the phlegm from her throat. "I can't stand out here all night."

Christ, the dog wasn't in sight.

Mistake, mistake, mistake, she thought, blowing her nose and trying to clear her sinuses yet again. Dog-sitting and her with a freaking summer cold and infected sinuses again. The timing couldn't have been worse.

"C'mon, dog," she called out into the dark night. "I'm freaking dying out here."

If Tiddles heard her, he was ignoring her. Damn mutt. In general, Melody liked furry creatures of all sorts but not when she was feeling like this and not when she was dog-sitting her sister's mutt—*what kind of fucking name was Tiddles anyway?*—and said mutt was a nasty little carpet-crawling Pomeranian that liked to nip fingers and pee on the rug and was only slightly less annoying than his master, Melody's sister Mimi. *He'll be no trouble. Trust me. You won't even know he's there.* But Melody knew all right, thank you very much, because she was standing out on the porch in the creeping dampness calling for him and if she'd forgotten he was there, he'd reminded her twice now by leaving presents on the kitchen floor. He was only lucky he was outside when she stepped in his latest pool of piss.

"Tiddles, c'mon already," she said, her head pounding.

Still, no dog.

Shit.

What now? It was times like these that she wished she were still married. This was the perfect errand to send a husband or a boyfriend out on so she could go back to bed. But she no longer had a husband because Skippo had screwed anything with a hole in the bottom and one of those holes had belonged to her best friend,

Kira. Scratch hubby and best friend off the list with one vivid red slash. And boyfriend? Fuck that. They were all the same. The only companion she needed took batteries and she put it back in the closet when she was done with it.

Enough, enough. When are you going to stop with that? Let it go.

She climbed into her tennies and went back out there with a flashlight. If something happened to the dog, Mimi was going to have a fucking stroke. She had a teenage daughter, too, but they didn't get along so well and a big part of that was the fact that she was second to Tiddles in Mimi's eyes.

Melody felt tense now.

She didn't really think she could feel worse than she did right now, but if that little mop got run down or ran away Mimi was going to freak. Melody, of course, had suggested a leash for when Tiddles had to go out and do his business, but Mimi wouldn't have that. *Tiddles doesn't like being tied up.* Melody told her there was sometimes heavy traffic on Birch after the bars closed at night. *No, Tiddles knows not to go out into the road.* But Melody wasn't so sure of that.

Sighing, she walked out to the street and played the light around, hoping she wasn't going to find a little doggie corpse or an ugly red smear on the pavement.

She found neither.

I told her he needed to be tied. She wouldn't listen.

"Tiddles," Melody called. "Tiddles?"

She went into the backyard and saw no sign of the dog. She even checked out in the alley and by the garbage cans to see if one of the neighborhood cats had beaten him down. Nothing. As she circled around the garage, she saw that the door was open. She must have forgotten to lock it. Sometimes it blew open if it wasn't secured.

She went in there and clicked the light on.

One of the bulbs was burned out, the other well on its way. Nothing much of interest. There was her bike. Her kayak in its bracket on the wall. Her rollerblades, a set of oars, her skis and poles, her snowboard. A few boxes of old clothes for Goodwill.

The recycling bin. A rack of shovels and rakes and brooms. A couple bags of empties and—

What the hell?

The walls were covered in tarpaper and the far wall just beyond the old cabinet where she kept paint and varnish and lawnmower oil was covered in glittering fragments. She'd never seen anything like it before. She got up close and saw that they looked like tiny shards of glass except that they were oddly star-shaped and spiky. All of them were imbedded in the tarpaper.

She couldn't figure it out.

They looked like some kind of weird, crystalline mineral deposits. But things like that didn't form over night. She was going to prod one with the flashlight, but decided maybe that wasn't such a good idea. She stopped, still trying to figure it all out and that's when she saw something shoved in between the old cabinet and the refrigerator the former owners had abandoned there when they moved.

The light was bad here, so she squinted her eyes and directed the flashlight beam into the crevice. Something white and shining. There was a weird smell coming off it. She went and grabbed a shovel, setting the flashlight aside.

She dug in there and pulled whatever it was out which turned out to be a tiny skeleton that broke apart as it hit the concrete floor.

Tiddles?

No, that was ridiculous. The dog had been outside for a couple of hours. You didn't waste away and turn to bone that quickly.

Melody stood there, shining the light on the bones that looked strangely old and pitted, discolored kind of like fossils. Her sinus condition was forgotten now. Her heart had picked up its rhythm and her back began to feel damp with sweat. It couldn't have been the dog, of course, but it certainly looked to be about the right size.

Like something fed on it, she thought then, *and stuffed its well-picked bones between the cabinet and refrigerator.*

That was ridiculous.

What could have fed on it? The only animals in the neighborhood were a couple of cats and a few squirrels. There was nothing else. And if something had fed on the dog, where was the blood? Where was the fur? There should have been something.

She found it a little far-fetched to believe that some nameless predator had devoured the dog, then, being tidy, had come into the garage to dispose of the skeleton.

But those bones.

Damn, they were the right size.

The *exact* size really and the skull looked very canine. Then again, she knew nothing of skulls. She would have been hard pressed to distinguish between the skull of a Pomeranian and a muskrat or a damn wombat when you came right down to it.

"Shit," she said under her breath.

It was the dog and she knew it was the dog. What other animal would have come in here to die? And if it had rotted away, she would have smelled it for weeks. Feeling afraid now, she began backing away towards the doorway. She was almost there when she heard someone come up behind her.

With a cry, she whirled around, raising the flashlight to strike.

"Easy," the voice said. "It's only me for chrissake."

Melody let out a long sigh, her body slumping. It was only Bobby Pistera from next door. Eighty if he was a day, he smiled and said, "Something got your goat tonight?"

"Yeah...I guess I'm a little tense," she said. "I'm looking for my sister's dog. I let him out earlier and he hasn't come back."

Bobby nodded. He fished a Camel from his pocket and snapped off the filter. "Funny sort of night," he said, lighting up. "That storm earlier. Sounded like hail falling. I looked out my window and I could see it coming down. Not like ordinary hail. Kind of shiny. Thought I heard people screaming out there when it fell."

"In the storm?"

"Yeah, weird. Of course, I'm old and I probably imagined it."

Melody realized that her robe was open a bit farther than it should have been and her left breast was trying to poke its way out like it wanted to say hi. Bobby had seen it, too. The boyish smirk on his face was evidence of that. She cinched the robe tighter, feeling embarrassed, feeling angry. Men, any men, that looked at her like that now left her feeling cold and militant inside.

They start out trying to be your friend. But that's just an excuse so they can ask you out. Which in itself is another sham because the entire time they're thinking about how soon they can screw you because that's all it really is with men—the dates, the flowers, the gifts, all of that silly romantic shit is just means to an end. It's how they lube you up before they—

Stop it! God! Move on!

Bobby pulled off his cigarette. "Funny night, all right. Thought...this is crazy," he said, blowing smoke out his nostrils, "but I thought I saw a guy walking down the street before. Looked like his hair was on fire."

Melody just stared at him. "On fire?"

"Course, I didn't have my specs on, so maybe I was seeing things."

People screaming in the storm, she thought, *and a man with his hair on fire.* That *was* crazy. She'd slept right through the storm, but what had happened since? Was it something that turned dogs to bones?

"I want to show you something," she said, making sure her robe was tight before she spoke. "It's over here."

Bobby followed her over to the cabinet and looked down at the bones. Carefully, as old people were wont to do, he kneeled down and looked at the now disarticulated skeleton. "Looks like a dog, I'd say, judging by those teeth." He stood up, shrugged. "Can't be your dog, though. That one's been dead for years, I'd say."

"But it wasn't there yesterday."

"Must have been."

"I'd have seen it."

Bobby pulled off his cigarette. "You saying something turned your little dog to bones since you let him outside earlier?"

Melody wasn't sure what to say. But, *yes,* that's exactly what she was thinking even though it made no sense whatsoever. "I don't know."

He just shrugged. "I'm pretty sure it's not your doggie, Melody."

She thought he was wrong...but what he said was perfectly rational so she wasn't about to argue with him. She took him over to the wall where the shards were. "What do you make of this?"

He got in closer. "Glass or something?"

"It wasn't there this morning. I know that much."

"Maybe you just didn't see it. If the light wasn't right, you know, you could've missed it."

Exasperated, she said, "Bobby, it wasn't here anymore than those bones were. Something weird's going on."

He just shrugged again which was no doubt his reaction to imaginative females who pranced about in the night with their tits hanging out.

"Catches the light like diamonds or something," he said, getting in even closer.

"Be careful. They look sharp."

She leaned against the cabinet while he looked them over. Finally he reached out and said, "Shit, they are sharp." Blood was running down his finger."

Boys will be boys, she thought.

But then something happened that made no sense. Bobby was standing there, examining his finger and he yelped. Something had cut his face and a trickle of blood ran down his cheek. "What the hell?" he said. And then he yelped again and this time Melody saw it happen: a shard of the stuff ejected from the wall and stuck in his forehead.

"Bobby?"

"It's…it's moving or something."

And it was. Those glistening, spiky shards seemed to be trembling. Another ejected and struck him, then another and another. "Jesus!" he cried out and before Melody could intervene, dozens of them shot out and struck him with more coming all the time. He was jerking and twisting as they pegged him, crying out and trying to cover his bleeding face. And as he did so, she saw one of them imbed itself into his forehead and…slide right into his skin.

"Bobby!"

"STAY BACK! STAY BACK!" he shouted as what seemed like hundreds of them hit him at once.

Melody fell back and almost went over.

Bobby went to his knees, shrieking and gasping. The remaining shards hit him. And all of them, she saw, slid right under his skin and so easily, so smoothly, it was like ice crystals melting on time-lapse.

He was on the floor, moaning and bleeding, opened in hundreds of minute gashes. His face was masked with blood. It came out of his eyes, his mouth, his ears, his scalp—in fact, everywhere.

"I'll get help!" Melody told him, running for the house, still overwhelmed by what she had just seen.

19

Out in the back parking lot of the Amoco station, Joe Sumner found that he was not alone. A woman came at him, making a whimpering sound in her throat. He stopped and backed away, figuring she was another of the infected.

It was just hard to tell.

She came towards him, stumbling and falling. She wore a leather blazer, plaid skirt, torn dark stockings, and a single shoe. She found her feet and staggered at him. "A girl...a thing," she managed. "It was in the street. It attacked me...it...it...*touched* me."

He heard that much of it anyway.

She was dirty and desperate, leaves in her hair, grime streaked over her face. One of her arms hung limply, the leather sleeve looking singed.

"Have to help me," she said, going down on her knees. "I'm...I'm Claire Stebbens...I...*I don't...don't know what the fuck is going on in this town!*"

Joe hesitated.

Did he help her or did he just get back to Susan? She was probably going nuts by this point. And if she got tired of waiting in the car and went into the station—

Oh Jesus!

"Listen," Joe said, reaching down and helping Claire to her feet. "I've got a car out front. We really need to get out of here right now. We don't have time to waste."

Claire nodded. She was mumbling things that made no sense whatsoever. Things about her husband and some guy named Derek and all manner of nonsense that he couldn't really understand. There was no time for it. Apparently, from what she was saying, she'd had a run-in with something that looked like a teenage girl but was in reality some kind of monster.

He didn't want to touch her because he was afraid she was infected with something, but there was simply no way he couldn't help her. She was desperate, at her wit's end. He *had* to help her.

He took her by the hand and started marching her around the front of the building and that's when the lights in the parking lot began to go out.

"Shit," he said.

Claire went stiff as a board, even the fingers of her hand were like pegs. She yanked free of him, started backing away. *"Oh...no, oh no...no...no...no..."* she said, shaking her head from side to side.

The lights dimmed until they were barely there and then came back on, though not as strongly. Their glow was sort of an anemic yellow that created too many shadows.

Joe grabbed Claire's hand again and she went wild, absolutely wild. She swung her fist at him, catching him in the cheekbone and then swinging again and again. He tried to ward off her blows, but she was fast and manic. She caught him in the head and the ear and then he knocked her hand away and shoved her back.

This was insane.

He had to get to Susan.

He didn't have time for a crazy woman.

Claire made a snarling sound and launched herself at him and he shoved her away again. "KNOCK IT OFF!" he cried at her. "KNOCK IT THE HELL OFF!"

Whatever had snapped in her, it had snapped but good. She reached out and seized his arm, her fingers pinching and painful, and he half-dragged her towards the front of the station. She was wild and screaming. He kept trying to throw her and when he did—tossing her through the air, her rump hitting the pavement— he almost wished he hadn't.

Because she was *claimed.*

The thing that had attacked her was back and Joe saw it in the dimming lights of the parking lot and let out an involuntary cry. It looked something like a girl, but it was no girl...at least, not one from this side of hell.

She stepped out of the shadows in a blasting cyclone of smoke and heat, a ghostly form crackling like a static discharge, her pallid sunken face set with two black holes for eyes that looked like cigarette burns in white rubber. Her toothless maw suctioned open and closed like some monstrous valve as she reached for Claire with fingers of white silk. A pale blue-white glow came from inside her, flickering through numerous cracks and crevices in her hide.

Claire screamed with volume, a real late night horror show kind of scream that made Joe's ears momentarily hurt.

But that was all she did.

By the time she found her feet, the girl grabbed her. Joe saw it happen as he backpedaled away. The girl's smoking fingers gripped Claire's shoulders and Claire screamed again...the fingers sizzling as they sank into her shoulders like hot blades into soft butter. Smoke and steam churned from her and blew out of her mouth in a burning mist. Her eyes bulged from their sockets and then exploded like slimy, rotten eggs as her skin blackened and curled from the skeleton below, her blood going to hot gas and the marrow boiled from her bones.

She let out a wild, agonized death cry that erupted from her mouth along with most of her teeth.

By the time the girl released her, Claire was a charred husk that seemed to explode as it hit the pavement, her ribcage breaking free and rolling at Joe's feet like a burning basket. A hot searing wind cast her ashes in all directions and then there was nothing left but scattered bones.

Then the girl moved towards Joe.

And by then he was running, his mind torn open like a puss-filled scab.

20

She hadn't even made it to the end of the block before Abby heard a tiny, extremely pathetic voice say, "Help me...please help me."

She stopped dead there, clutching baby Megan to her. Her first responsibility was to herself and the baby. She was in no position to be playing hero or savior, but that voice, that poor voice.

"Please help me," the voice said again, only this time it was even more pitiable than before.

Abby sighed. *You should have kept going. You're just asking for trouble.* And it wasn't too late to do that, she knew. Just walk away. *I can't do that.* She turned and called into the shadows, "Who's there?"

A little boy stepped out, still wearing his footed Dr. Denton's. From what Abby could see of him in the moonlight, he was no more than four. A little blonde-haired kid with big eyes and a look of abject terror to him. She thought she kind of half-recognized him. She'd seen him out in the yard of a Cape Cod on the corner with a woman who she knew was Mrs. Pajo, who was a teacher of some sort at the high school.

"What's your name?" she asked.

"Denny."

"Denny Pajo?"

He nodded. "Okay, I'm Abby. Where's your mom and dad?"

He started to sob, telling her in a broken voice that people had come into their house and when they left, his mom and dad were gone and there were just skeletons in their bed, skeletons like at Halloween.

Poor kid. His own mom and dad yet.

"Okay, come with us. We're going someplace that's safe. We have to be quiet."

Denny didn't seem to understand that concept, however, and started pelting her with questions. "How old are you?"

"Sixteen."

"Is that your baby?"

"No, I'm just sitting her."

"Sitting on her?"

"No, *baby*sitting her. Now keep up with me and be quiet. We have to be real quiet."

He fell into silence and she was glad for that because more than anything she needed to listen for the things out there. There were more of them and she knew it. Now she was responsible for not only baby Megan but for this little boy. It was up to her to get them somewhere safe.

Denny began to sob.

"What's wrong?" she asked.

"I'm scared."

"Me, too, but we'll be okay as long as we're quiet."

"Goob?" Megan said.

Abby sighed.

Denny started to giggle despite himself.

They made it to the end of the block, pausing there, quite near Denny's house, just waiting and watching. Everything seemed quiet. Abby saw nothing and heard nothing...yet, she had the worst sort of feeling that they were not alone.

21

When Charlie Shaw finally made it home, he saw that the lights were on in the kitchen and the TV was glowing in the living room. Candy was still up then. She was waiting up for him as she did some nights, usually because she had a funny story from work or her sister had pissed her off again. Standing there on the walk, covered in sweat from his run and knowing he was too damn old to be sprinting across town like a teenager, he waited a moment or two while he caught his breath. His heart was beating hard and his head felt all bleary from the exertion, his face red and hot.

But I made it, he thought. *I goddamn well made it.*

When his heart slowed and his breathing returned to near normal, he cast a wary eye around the neighborhood and climbed the porch to the front door. Candy had the inside door open. He opened the screen door and it screeched like usual, a sound which seemed glaringly loud tonight.

He headed into the kitchen. "Candy!" he cried out before he was even in there. "Candy!"

But the kitchen was empty...empty save for a dirty trail coming in through the wide open back door. It was black and wet, almost slimy-looking with mud and grass clippings and even a few stray leaves. It looked like a giant slug had left it.

"Candy?" he said, his concern beginning to rise again.

It looked like she had dragged something heavy along the floor or dragged herself. As he looked down at the trail, he noticed a dusting of those same luminous particles he'd seen at Rick Pacek's house.

Oh no, oh Christ.

He went into the living room at a pretty good clip and saw that Candy was sitting in her recliner, watching TV in the dark. She just sat there, the images on the screen flickering like an old newsreel.

"Candy?" he said, his concern becoming a tension in his chest that escalated into hot fingers of fear as she did not move, did not do anything. God knew, he didn't expect her to leap up like a dog when he walked into the house but usually she said something or got up and started chatting.

He went over to her. "Candy? Are you awake? Are you…awake?"

She sat there like a waxworks dummy and in the blue glow of the TV, he saw that she was bloodless-looking, her face set with ragged black holes. And she had no eyes.

"Candy!" he shouted, grabbing hold of her and instantly regretting it. The initial contact seared his hand and made him cry out. Her arm was hotter than a steam pipe. A split second after he'd touched her—in fact before he could even withdraw his hand—a surge of current slammed into him and threw him five feet where he crashed into the TV, nearly flipping it off the stand. His hand was smoking, the flesh hanging in tatters, the pain unbelievable.

Candy just sat there, staring off at the wall with empty eye sockets. Then she began to tremble and quake. Smoke rose from her hair in pale white wisps. It came from her eyes and ears and the punctures in her face. Her toothless mouth opened like a black, sucking wound, a huge cloud of blue-white smoke came rolling out as if she had just pulled from a cigar.

The smell of Charlie's scalded flesh mixed with the distinctive and nauseating odor of seared meat, burnt hair, and something like melted circuitry and blown fuses.

As he writhed there on the floor, he saw Candy stand up, more smoke rising from her and forming a roiling fog above her head. It seemed to blow out of her. She pushed a wave of furnace heat before her and he could feel it against his face, burning as if he was too close to a bonfire.

He pulled himself up with his good hand, the room seeming to whirl around him. His knees were rubbery, his face corded with pain. The agony was so intense he had to clench his teeth to keep from crying out.

"Candy," he said in a moaning voice that became a whimpering. *"Oh, Candy…oh not you…oh, dear God, not you…"*

The lights in the kitchen were flickering. The TV picture rolling faster and faster. And then the screen blew right out with a resounding *crack!* The kitchen lights went out completely and Charlie was in the dark with the thing that had once been his wife.

Though he knew he mustn't make any sound, there was just no way he couldn't. He tripped over his own feet, he bumped into the wall, he smacked his bad hand off the edge of a table in the hallway and screamed at the onslaught of pain.

Candy was coming.

She was right behind him, making a crackling sort of sound like coals popping in a fire pit. He heard a whooshing noise and the entire wall across from him exploded with flames. He went down to one knee, the heat singeing his eyebrows. He looked back and Candy was coming on, her hands reaching out for him, her fingers on fire like lantern mantles. They blazed and sputtered. Her mouth was a flame-blackened cavity yawning wide.

He stumbled on, getting away from her and the flames, falling to one knee again and an orange-yellow gout of fire passed just over his head, lighting his hair up and igniting the curtains in the dining room.

He screamed, slapping at his head with his good hand, the stink of burnt hair like a pall around him.

In the light of the blaze, he saw Candy shuffling in his direction, still smoldering and smoking. Her lips had been burned away as was most of her lower face, tongues of flame flickering from her gums like gas jets. Then her mouth opened wider, her face cracking open, and a directed, gushing river of fire came out.

There was no way to avoid it.

Charlie was caught in a mushrooming ball of flames that engulfed him, burning away his eyelids and making his lips split open like sausages. He fought and screamed, slamming into the wall and writhing on the floor as he slowly burned alive, his eyes superheating and blowing from their sockets, his flesh cracking open, his lungs crystallizing from the intense heat.

Within five minutes as his corpse sputtered and popped, the house was burning. Candy—or the hell-wraith she now was—stood there and watched it burn. She was on fire herself, her flesh melting in runnels that oozed from her face, bubbling and steaming. A living corpse-oven ablaze with dancing fire-ghosts that haunted her and chewed the meat from her bones with hot, hungry mouths until her blackened bones fell to the floor and the house trembled and split, coming down on her in an orange, fiery mass, sealing her in a crypt of hot embers and blowing red sparks.

22

The wind was decidedly warmer as Tommy McCleesh squealed his taxicab to a halt before the Middleburg Police Station, hopping out—nearly falling out—before it had come to a complete stop. He saw lights on in the station and if there was anybody who might know what the hell was going on it was the police.

As he dashed up the sidewalk to the steps of the station, he heard a drawn-out piercing shriek coming from inside. That stopped him and left him standing there with his skin crawling.

Shit.

The lights in the police station flickered, went out, then came back on again.

He heard the scream yet again and bolted up the steps, wondering exactly what he was stepping into here and knowing it was probably the same thing that had happened at Barred & Bottled. Only this time, he was going to *see* it happening, rather than the aftermath of it.

He heard more cries and the distinct popping of an automatic as somebody fired off a few rounds.

He either went in there now and found out what was going on, a decidedly dicey proposition at best, or he just got the hell out.

There was no decision.

He went in and wrinkled his nose at the burning stink that filled the building. It was a raging, hot sort of smell that made him pause indecisively there in the entry. He heard another scream, then a couple of shouting voices that sounded like they came from men completely out of their minds.

"GET BACK! GET BACK! GET THE FUCK AWAY FROM ME!"

He started down a long corridor studded with doors and set with community announcement corkboards on them. More gunfire and damn close now. Another scream cycled up, echoing through the building, rising into a shrill screech of pain and terror as if its owner was being peeled with a hot knife. A door burst open and a body hit the floor twenty feet from him.

Jesus H. Christ...

It was burning.

Its hands scraped over the floor, fingers like crumbling black sticks breaking apart on the tiles. It looked in his direction with a seared black mask and then stopped moving, choking fumes rising from it in acrid clouds.

Tommy backed up, gasping, hanging onto the wall.

Breathing hard, he approached the doorway, stepping around the blackened thing on the floor. He peered into the room and saw it was a bullpen of sorts. Everything was in disarray. Chairs were tipped over, papers scattered. There were bullet holes in the walls along with dark streaks and black handprints, one of which was still hot enough to be smoking. But the real tragedy were the squirming things on the floor that had once been men and women and were now cremated shells, struggling in their death throes.

There was a gun on the floor, a Beretta 9mm and Tommy took it, knowing it probably wouldn't do him much good, but relieved to have a weapon of any sort in his hand.

He stepped lightly through the room, staring out the broken windows, expecting to see faces like fright masks looking back in at him, but seeing nothing.

Take a quick look for survivors. Then find the radio. They've got to have a radio here somewhere.

The air was filled with smoke and the smell was gagging. He actually paused, leaning on a desk and coughing. It was that bad. He heard another scream and it seemed to come from deeper in the complex, echoing through the building.

He knew the reasonable and safe thing was to turn back and get out while he could, but a morbid curiosity pushed him forward. It wanted him to see. It wanted him to know just how bad this could be, to rub his nose in it, so he pushed forward into the next room and found another dead cop.

The others were bad enough, but this one he had to turn away from. It looked initially like the officer in question was leaning against the wall, but he wasn't leaning there, he was *melted* into it. As horrifying as it was, there was something grimly fascinating about the sort of energy it would have taken to fuse a human body and cheap veneer paneling into a single mass. The cop leaned there, little more than a skeleton adhered to the wall behind it by the gummy remains of its own flesh that spread out in tendrils and ropes like runnels and spreading fingers of wax.

These cops have been slaughtered, he thought. *Do you really think you stand a chance?*

No, he didn't think that at all.

He was fucked four ways to Sunday, but yet he kept going, tracking the horror to its source, his anxiety rising and his terror spiking as his blood pressure nearly went through the roof.

He didn't find what he was looking for until he got into the back of the building. Across the hallway from a lunchroom where a couple of skeletons hunched over a table looking as if they'd vomited their anatomy into a central, oozing pool, there was a couple holding cells. These, Tommy knew, were used to hold the bad boys overnight before their trip to the county lockup.

As soon as he got in there, the lights began dimming, threatening to go out. The idea of being trapped inside the police station in the dark was unthinkable. As they went out, he saw something that sent him running—in one of the cells, he saw a figure, a shape, something nightmarish that looked like a woman…sort of. She was a ghostly figure with the translucent skin of a moonstone. Energy pulsated from within her in an eerie effulgence, lighting up her insides like an x-ray, giving him a three-dimensional view of her skeleton which flickered on and off like a bulb that was about to burn out. She was holding onto a man with a hand to each side of his face and he was superheating, smoking and crackling like a green log in a fire. His skin split open like the greasy casing of a sausage and the flesh beneath ran like grease.

It seemed to take seconds.

He dropped to the floor, spluttering and hissing, and the woman turned her face towards Tommy.

That's when the lights really went out.

But it didn't matter because the energy inside her ignited her with a weird sort of coruscation and lit up the room with strobing light, creating a macabre show of shadows that crawled over the walls. Her face glowed like a jack-o-lantern with a candle burning inside it, bluish incandescence flashing from the puckering oval of her toothless mouth and the depthless hollows of her eyes.

Screaming and unable to stop himself from doing so, Tommy brought up the 9mm and capped three rounds into her and the only effect it had was to open up more holes in her skin from which that surreal blue glow spoked out.

He stumbled back out into the corridor, retracing his steps, feeling her coming up behind him, slowly but relentlessly.

When he made it back outside, he went down to one knee and vomited. The stink, the sights, the terror overwhelmed him.

And when it passed, he made for the cab but he never got there because there were a dozen more of those things in the street, reaching out for him with white melting fingers.

23

It was no good, of course. The landline was down and Melody couldn't get anything from her cell. She made a good effort of it, though. She tried and tried again before she simply gave up and ran back out to the garage and by then Bobby was dead.

At least, he wasn't moving.

"Bobby?" she said when she got in there, shivering from head to toe because she knew he was far beyond help.

He didn't reply, of course, or do anything for that matter. He laid there like a corpse neatly trimmed in red lace, a leaking battle-worn ship sinking into a bloody sea. The red stuff had come out of holes and lacerations too numerous to count. There wasn't enough tar in the world to seal up the old leaky barge of Bobby Pistera and the ocean within him.

She just stood there in her robe, feeling foolish and hopeless, thinking that only an hour before she had been sleeping. Then the dog went missing. Then she found the shards and the bones. Then Bobby showed up and then and then—

That's where things got crazy.

That's what she was having trouble with.

That's what made her feel like a glass that had been upended and poured out.

But I saw them, she thought. *I saw those shards fire out of the wall. I saw it.*

They had exploded free like corks from wine bottles and there had been no mistaking that they sought Bobby out like they were living things. She had clearly seen them not only stick in him, but slide beneath his skin like razor blades. As if that had been their goal, to get inside him.

But that's not possible, it's just not possible.

She had to turn away from him because she was sick to her stomach, feeling light-headed and more than a little woozy. She stepped out of the garage and tried to think, tried to make sense of this.

Bobby said hail had fallen.

Not ordinary hail, but shiny hail.

People were screaming.

A guy walked by with his hair on fire.

Then the dog bones.

The *living* shards.

And now Bobby was dead and Melody felt like she was adrift on a very big ocean in a very small raft without so much as a paddle. What did she do now? There was a body in her garage. Without a phone, what the hell was she supposed to do?

Standing there, she could smell smoke like somebody had a bonfire going. Only it was much stronger. In the distance, she could see an orange glow. God, was the town on fire?

Behind her, there was a groaning.

Bobby?

He groaned again, the fingers of his left hand trembling slightly. He wasn't dead. He really wasn't dead. Somehow, some way there was still life struggling in him. The idea seemed fantastic, but there it was.

"Bobby, try not to move," she told him. "I'll get some help."

She dashed out through the door, scolding herself for standing around and getting nothing done while the poor old guy was fighting for his life. Not that she was surprised for she had made a career out of fiddling while Rome burned.

Still wearing really nothing more than a robe and tennies, she ran out front, feeling the dry heat that seemed to be blowing down the street. Over in the direction of King Street, she could see a guttering orange glow that was far too bright to be anything less than a house on fire.

But she heard no sirens.

Was no one else seeing this?

She was simply exasperated and bewildered by this night. It was as if reality had been turned on its head and reconfigured into something much darker. Wherever she looked for it, it seemed to be missing or it lifted its skirts and mooned her.

What the fuck is going on? Is everyone dead? Did the world come to an end and somebody forgot to tell me?

There was no time for that. She needed help. Maybe the phones were down, but if she could help, maybe they could get

Bobby into a truck or a van and over to the hospital in North Platte. She couldn't do it alone and she sure as hell couldn't fit an injured man into her little Mazda Miata. The house next door was empty, but the house down the way belonged to the Zims. They were both elderly, but Mr. Zim had a big old gas-guzzling SUV that would be perfect for the job.

Melody ran past the house next door and came around the hedges that separated it from the Zim house. Ducking beneath a big, spreading weeping willow, she cut through the yard and stopped about ten feet from the wraparound porch.

Someone was there.

Someone was sitting in the rocking chair Mrs. Zim whiled away her summer afternoons in. They were rocking back and forth seemingly without a care in the world.

In the moonlight, Melody could see that it was, in fact, Mrs. Zim herself. The momentary anxiety she felt lessened by degrees.

"Mrs. Zim?" she said, putting one foot up on the lowest porch step but unwilling to go any farther. "I need help! Bobby Pistera is hurt. Phones are down. We need to get him to the hospital!"

Mrs. Zim kept rocking.

Melody, her anxiety becoming a slow-turning dread, tried to swallow and found that she couldn't. "Mrs. Zim? *Mrs. Zim?*"

The figure kept rocking and rocking with a slow and easy rhythm. There was something unbearably eerie about that here in the dead of night and Melody felt a trickle of sweat slide down her left temple even as a cold shiver ran up her back. Something was terribly wrong here. Mrs. Zim was like some kind of wind-up doll rocking back and forth. She reminded her of the mechanical figures at House on the Rock in Wisconsin—you'd walk into a dim room and the band would start playing. The figures would look real until you got close and saw they were clockwork dolls. There was something unbelievably creepy about them and there was something unbelievably creepy about Mrs. Zim.

Melody removed the foot she had placed on the lowest step. In fact, she moved back a few feet, a formless terror running wild inside her.

"Mrs. Zim?" she said, practically choking on her own words.

You can call her name all night, but she won't respond because she's not exactly human any more.

The idea of that was ridiculous, but Melody accepted it without any doubt.

Mrs. Zim kept rocking, only now a scratching sound was coming from inside her and it sounded very much like someone striking a match. Melody could even smell something like sulfur. It burned her nostrils. She heard the scratching again followed by a sort of crackling sound like dry branches under a boot.

Then there was a flash of light.

Mrs. Zim had ignited.

Flames engulfed her and she wore them like a burning shroud, in blazing veils of orange and yellow. The housecoat she wore was on fire. Her hair was on fire. Flames swarmed over her like infesting fire-hot insects. Still she rocked, back and forth, back and forth, content in her incineration.

Melody screamed.

It came unbidden and shrill, rushing out of her with volume as she stared with unblinking eyes at the burning woman. Like a witch blazing on a stake, she superheated, something like hot pitch running from her in sizzling rivers. Her face was warm clay sliding from the bones below. Clouds of churning black smoke rose from her, dancing about like ghosts and exhaling breaths of crematory ash. She began to split open like a natural casing wiener roasted on a stick, revealing a superhot blue core within her that looked oddly crystalline like the shards that had imbedded themselves in Bobby Pistera. It hissed and snapped and was replaced by something bright red that looked like seams of lava seen through cracks in the earth's crust.

Still, she rocked on, back and forth.

By then, the porch had caught on fire and Melody, whimpering and out of her head, stumbled back to get away from the heat. She saw Mrs. Zim melt like a wax doll, becoming a bubbling river of liquid flesh that dripped to the porch in pools of hot grease.

Only then did the chair stop rocking when her blackened bones collapsed in an untidy heap amongst the flames. As Ray Bradbury had said, it was a pleasure to burn.

24

Abby began to question what it was she was doing and how she could possibly hope to accomplish it. Cradling Megan to her with her left arm and holding Denny's hand, she paused there, thinking, plotting, scheming even. There was a lot at stake here. It amazed her in the worst possible way that in the past few hours she had been forced from being a more or less self-indulgent, self-infatuated teenager—something she didn't like to admit— to an adult that had to protect two children.

The responsibility of that was staggering.

What was going on?

Why weren't the police doing something?

And why was she caught in the middle of it?

She just stood there, listening, knowing that she had to make the right decisions and terrified that she might make the wrong ones and doom all of them.

"Just use your head," she told herself in a whisper.

"What?" Denny whispered back.

"Nothing. Just thinking out loud."

She stood there another few moments, head cocked, ears perked, mind reaching out as if to catch some psychic whiff of oncoming danger.

"Okay, onward," she told Denny, feeling his warm fingers nervously kneading the back of her hand.

She walked on…then stopped.

Something just felt wrong here. It would have taken her twenty minutes to adequately catalog what it was, but it was there and it was real—a presentment of danger. It buzzed inside her head like flies in a jelly jar.

She started walking again, but slowly, putting each foot down with great care. Denny was feeling it, too, and he tensed beside her. Megan began to squirm.

Up ahead, hidden from view by a dark wall of bushes, she saw a vague flicker of light that was there and then gone.

Listen.

A humming sound now like something was being powered up. It was near-constant like the humming of power lines at midsummer. Now she began to see strobing blue flashes like someone was taking shots with an old Kodak using a flashbulb.

They were coming.

She grabbed Denny and pulled him behind the bushes. When he opened his mouth to say something, she silenced him with an index finger to her lips. She smelled a burnt sort of stink that got stronger and stronger. She heard shuffling footsteps pass and saw a glimmering, unnatural incandescence. Then it was gone and she was breathing again.

How many of those damn things were there?

Back on the sidewalk, they started walking again. Not quickly, but surely. They were moving and that was the important part.

They walked on maybe another ten minutes and Denny said, "Hey! The police!"

But Abby had already scoped what he was looking at. A police cruiser was parked in the middle of the road. And she wasn't so sure that *parked* was the proper word here, because it looked abandoned. One of the doors was open. From where she was, she couldn't tell if there was anyone in there or not.

Well, do I or don't I? If the radio's working, I could call for help.

And what if no one answered?

That's really what she was afraid of. The very idea that she was the last—or one of the last—people in town scared the hell out of her.

She supposed she should have made Denny hold Megan while she went over there and snooped, but she did not dare let the baby out of her sight for even a minute. So she went over there and Denny followed her. She wanted to call out, but she knew the folly of attracting unwanted attention.

When she was about fifteen feet from the cruiser, the strangest thing happened: there was a popping sort of sound and something like a ripple of pulsating blue fire enveloped the car. It passed very quickly, but made a crackling sound of static like the sort that might come from a microphone.

She waited a moment and nothing else happened. Then, closer, she saw another discharge of blue energy. It seemed to break against the front of the cruiser like a wave, sending eddies and glowing twisters along its length.

Go figure that one.

She got in a little closer, her mouth dry and her heart rattling like a snare drum. Another current of energy passed over the car and this time, she could feel the static charge over her bare arm. Up close like that, but maintaining a respectable safety margin of ten feet, she could see that smoke was billowing out of the open door. It brought a harsh, ashy sort of stink with it. When the energy pulsed again, she could plainly see someone sitting in the driver's seat and they looked very much like Mrs. Pearson had—a cremated husk that was still burning, popping like a roasting ear of corn, letting off foul plumes of dirty smoke. Every time it made that popping noise, bits of it crumbled away, ashes spilling out the door and to the street below.

Abby pulled Denny away and they made a wide berth around the front of the cruiser. She saw then that the other door was open, too, but there was no one sitting on that side. The air was rank with the caustic, bitter stench of cooking transformers.

And she saw why.

There on the ground was a bone. She thought it might be a tibia. In the moonlight, it looked brown and split open. A few feet away was another bone, a femur. Then a pelvic girdle, some scattered vertebrae, half a smoldering ribcage, a scapula, an outstretched radius and some scattered metacarpals, and finally, a jawless skull, oily smoke still rising from its eye sockets. All of it blown by gray ash. It looked like whoever it had been, they were falling apart as they tried to crawl away from the cruiser.

She saw something shining on the pavement and realized it was a silver badge that had been melted.

Denny started to sob.

Megan decided to join in.

Abby had a very strong desire to do the same. She turned away, thinking how the bones of someone that had died violently were so much different than the white antiseptic skeleton hanging in Bio II classroom, a.k.a. "Boney Maroney."

She mellowed out Megan easy enough, but Denny started to sob louder until it became a wailing that sounded as loud as a siren in the stillness of night.

"Stop it," she told him, trying to find some sympathy inside her and realizing she was fresh out. "Knock it off."

Maybe it was the tone in her voice, but he quieted almost immediately and it was then that she heard that humming noise again. It was dull and seemingly distant at first, but now steadily rising into a fever pitch, becoming high and droning like the buzz of a fly.

"Abby!" Denny cried out.

She wanted to warn him to be quiet, but it was too late. Two of the things came out of the darkness, shrunken and cadaverous and crawling with a minute emanation of blue light. Steam blew off them in rolling clouds, their bones straining against the vellum-thin covering of their skin. Their lips were peeled back, but they had no teeth anymore than they had eyes.

They came right at her, both of them simultaneously lifting a hand in her direction as if they wanted to shake on the deal. One was a man and the other was a woman, not that it mattered.

Abby led Denny away into the shadows, breaking into a run when they reached the sidewalk, leaving the things far behind them.

25

There was a method to this madness, it occurred to Tommy McCleesh as he leaned up against a shed in the shadows, trying to get control of himself before blind panic caused him to make a very, very bad mistake. There were about a dozen of those things—he called them *fire-eaters*—gathered out in the street and they were looking for him. Their tell-tale blue-gray effulgence created an unearthly, spectral light show that lit off the faces of houses, creating a weird nightscape of crawling shadows. Trees became clutching hands, homes crooked leaning headstones, and the fire-eaters themselves distorted creeping forms. It reminded him of an old spooky black-and-white cartoon.

Well, what's your plan? You can't just hide here all night. Sooner or later, they're going to find you. Maybe they can't see you, but you know they can hear you.

Part of him was all for crouching down there in the darkness by the shed and waiting things out. That was a pretty safe bet. He didn't know exactly what was going on, save that the good people of Middleburg had become monsters and the town was under siege.

That's all he really knew.

And, realistically, all he had to know.

The idea of hiding like a frightened mouse wasn't very appealing. He kept hoping the police or somebody would roll in and clean this mess up, but after what he'd seen at the station he didn't think that was going to happen.

But somebody's gotta be moving on this. A town can't fall off the map. Somebody somewhere must have sounded the alarm. And the State Patrol are going to get suspicious if there's nothing coming out of Middleburg...aren't they?

Tommy didn't know what to think.

His original idea had been to make his way back to the cabstand and get in his car and hightail right out of town. That still sounded like the most feasible idea. Just waiting here like this, hoping for help that might not be coming, and praying that when the sun came up this nightmare would end was just not a reasonable course of action.

He lit a cigarette, wondering if they had heard his Zippo. If they had, they gave no indication of the same. Some of them were moving about, but most were just standing stock-still out there in the middle of the street as if they were waiting for something.

No, not waiting but *listening.*

He pulled off his cigarette and felt around in the grass. He found a couple sticks but they weren't heavy enough to throw. He found a stone, small but weighty. He tossed it out there and it hit the trunk of a car and rolled into the street. A couple of them moved in that direction, but in a slow almost disinterested sort of way.

Now what?

"Don't fucking ask me," he said out loud in frustration, immediately realizing that he had broken the silence and they were aware of it.

Now, five or six of them had entered the yard and were moving in his direction. *Good going.* He tossed his cigarette and climbed slowly to his feet. They were bearing down on him, moving faster than he thought possible.

Go!

He was on the run again. He dashed through one yard, then another, hopping a fence and cutting between two houses. He paused there, breathing hard more out of fear than exertion. He saw flickering lights coming from two different directions. He did not wait to see what they came from. He moved again. He ran down another street, cut through two more yards, and shot into an alley that was hemmed in by a high stone wall on one side and a wrought-iron fence on the other.

It was dark in there, terribly dark.

So dark he did not dare to plunge blindly down its length in case there were fire-eaters waiting for him. Usually you could see the weird light they threw, but not always.

He swallowed, fear gathering in his chest like moths circling a streetlight. He wiped sweat from his face, moving carefully forward to the lit street on the other side. There were hulking dark shapes around him that he navigated with great caution in case one of them came alive. He threaded his way with deliberate vigilance, the light at the end getting closer and closer.

Easy as pie, he told himself.

But as they always said, it's the bullet you don't hear that kills you and the thing you never see coming that trips you up. Which made perfect sense when he walked right into a metal garbage can, overturning it and sending its lid rolling for five feet where it clattered to a stop.

Shit.

Shit was right because he now saw a flickering light coming from behind him. He pressed himself against the stone wall, looking back. There were several of them at the mouth of the alley. They were not moving, just standing there like sentries. One more noise, regardless how minor, would bring them. Regulating his breathing, lips pressed tight, he began inching his way down the alley, his back still pressed up against the wall. He kept moving like that—one light and careful step after the other—like a kid walking a high ledge.

Five feet.

The fire-eaters still had not moved.

Ten feet.

Still as stone.

Twenty feet.

They looked like statues down there.

Then, with a dread that bottomed him right out and emptied him like a balloon pricked with a pin, he saw another form moving down the alley from the opposite direction. In the pale moonlight, he could see it had the general form of a woman…but it was no woman.

It began throwing out an arc of blue light.

It crept ever forward with a sort of hissing sound like a leaky valve. The further it came into the alley, the more light it seemed to radiate. Whether that was just because the dark made it seem so, he did not know.

He waited there, his entire body trembling.

She was on the opposite side of the alley, moving down the wrought-iron fence. She dragged the fingers of one hand against it and they made a popping sound at each upright, a popping sound and a flicker of light like a struck match head. *Pop, pop, pop.* She was closer now. When she was no more than fifteen feet from him, she paused and cocked her head as if maybe she could hear his breathing. She gripped the wrought-iron fence with one hand and reached out into the darkness with the other as if she was feeling the air.

Tommy waited there, sweat rolling down his face in salty beads that broke against his lips.

She knew he was near, just not exactly where.

More of that glow was spiking from her now as if she were getting excited. He could see that she was split open in many places, her hot luminous blue core revealed. It lit up her face in strobing bursts of illumination, enough so that he could see it was barely a face. It looked like a sloughing rubber mask hanging in flaps and ribbons from the skull beneath.

Something else was happening now.

As she held that hand out, moving it back and forth, the fingers were pulsating with an energetic flow that ran right up her arm. There was a sound like stretching rubber, then a ripping noise like tearing canvas and sharp little protrusions began to jut out from her flesh. It was most noticeable at her face…glimmering spikes, what seemed hundreds of them protruding like the thorns of a rose stem, save these were translucent and glasslike reminding him of mineral growths.

What the fuck is this shit now?

As the spikes or shards erupted from her, she continued to make the ripping noise and that crackling sound, gouts of hot steam rising from her. The stink of it was sulfurous like gunpowder.

And hot.

Waves of blistering heat emanated from her, cycling out at him and making his face burn and his clothes cling with sweat to him like damp rags.

She took a step towards him and something inside him just broke. Whatever was holding him together up to that point just snapped and he let out a shrill cry and ran.

But just before he did, he saw her raise both arms up revealing dozens upon dozens of those shards sticking out from the undersides like splinters of shattered ice.

Then he moved.

And not a second too soon, because those shards ejected from her arms like projectiles, hitting the wall where he had just been. He looked back only once and saw her slowly turning in his direction. But that wasn't what scared him, but the fact that those shards were imbedded right into the stone wall.

Choking down a scream of madness, his feet pounded off into the night.

26

When Joe Sumner made it around the front of the station, he saw that Susan was outside the car, staring in glaze-eyed fascination at the station itself. He saw why. The lights were off in there but there was a guttering radiance lighting up the place in irregular flashes. With each burst of illumination, he saw a figure getting closer to the plate glass doors, which, like the windows to either side of them, became discolored with dark streaks as if they were being exposed to incredible heat. Then they were not just smudged but black.

The door and the windows simply shattered like candy glass.

He saw someone standing by the pumps. Someone not strictly human. It was what they did that totally floored him. They raised the nozzle and put it between their lips, squeezing the trigger. Gasoline filled their mouth and splashed over them, spreading in a pool at their feet.

They were drinking it.

No, no, no, this couldn't be fucking happening. He was not seeing these things, but apparently Susan saw it, too, because her mouth was hanging open.

"Get in the car!" Joe screamed at her. *"Hurry! Get in the fucking car! We have to get out of here!"*

Susan jumped in without any further prodding and Joe was squealing out of the lot before her door was even closed. She looked dazed in the dash lights, more so, stunned. She fumbled her seatbelt into place and locked it down, but still did not speak. Not even when they roared out into the street and there were a dozen of those zombielike apparitions moving about with outstretched hands.

"We have to get home," Joe told her. "We have to get to Megan before..."

"Before what?" she said.

But he just shook his head because he did not know. He just did not know. He drove, keeping a close eye on the dash lights and headlights, whenever they began to dim, he cut off in another direction. They went down streets and avenues, veering sharply into narrow alleys. More than once, he pulled U-turns right in the middle of the road.

What alarmed him the most was that he never saw another vehicle.

"What the heck's going on?" Susan said after a time, the shock that had shut her down releasing her.

"I don't know, but we have to get home and get Megan and get the hell out of here."

She nodded as if that made perfect sense, but he had a pretty good idea that none of it was really sinking in. Not just yet. Regardless, he was glad she didn't ask him any questions because he simply did not have answers.

He drove for another five minutes, taking a very roundabout route that added a great deal of time, and finally she said, "What the hell's going on, Joe? Who are those people? What are they doing?"

"I don't know, but they're crazy. I think they're infected with something."

That got a little gasp from her and maybe gruesome images of Ebola and plague were dancing through her head.

Infected? he asked himself. *Yes. Maybe. Possibly. But not in the ordinary way.*

This wasn't a virus or a bacterium. It was no deadly germ. What it was exactly, he did not know. He only understood a few things and that was whatever had happened to those people, they were like some kind of ghouls now. Their presence dimmed lights and they burned up whatever they touched. That wasn't much but it was all he really had to know.

"We need to get to Megan," Susan said then. *"Joe!* We need to get to Megan."

"That's where we're going."

"Hurry," she said.

He watched the old familiar neighborhoods wing by, only they had changed now. What had once been familiar was now alien and what had once been commonplace was now frightening.

He came down a street, a bare four blocks from home, and there were five or six of them blocking the way. Right away, the headlights began to dim as did the dash lights. He threw the VW in reverse and squealed out of there, popping a curb and spinning out in the dew on someone's lawn. He cut down the way they had come, hung a right…and hit the brakes.

There were at least ten of them in the street ahead, closing in on them.

"Please, Joe, just get us home," Susan said.

God knew it was what he wanted but it wasn't quite that easy. It would probably have been easier on foot. He steered the car down an alley, the tires crunching over scattered bones that neither of them commented on. When he pulled out into the adjoining street—Placer Drive, he thought—he knew they were now farther from home than they had been just a few minutes before. It was madness. Absolute madness.

"Why aren't the police or National Guard doing something about this?" Susan said.

"I'd like to know that myself," he told her.

She tried calling 911 again, but got only static as before.

He drove on, finding a clear path and picking up speed. He crossed Main Street and saw more of the things walking around and then squealed to a halt not a block away. There were two cars in the middle of the street, abandoned. There was no way to get around them. He started backing up and the lights dimmed and went out.

"Joe!" Susan cried.

He tried turning over the VW again and again, but it was simply no good. They weren't going anywhere and the reason for that became quickly apparent: the things were all around them. They were pushing in from every side, hordes of them. Their combined presence must have knocked out the car's electrical system in a flash. Much faster than he could have hoped to react.

Susan screamed, dropping her cell and fighting with her belt.

"We're safe in here!" Joe told her, even though he did not know it to be true.

The ghouls pressed in closer and now he could see their white ghost faces punctured with dark holes and crevices, their empty eye sockets, mouths opening and closing, and their smoldering fingers that reached towards the car. Inside, the stroboscopic effect of their nearness made everything seem to move in slow motion.

He heard Susan scream, but there wasn't a damn thing he could do about it. One of them reached through the window for her with a gnarled, steaming hand, the nails looking black as if they were burnt. It didn't break the window; its hand passed right *through* the glass as if it was made of fog. The glass darkened, but did not come apart. The hand bisected it quite easily with a hissing sort of sound, burning its way straight through.

Then it seized Susan.

She went rigid, straining against her seatbelt, eyes bugging from her head and her mouth peeled open in a weak, watery sort of scream. Smoke billowed from her and there was cracking/snapping sound from inside her that sounded oddly like popping corn. Blood bubbled from her nostrils and sprayed from her mouth. Her skin darkened and split open, her eyes superheating and hissing before exploding and ejecting against the windshield like squashed slugs. Then steaming tissue gushed from the sockets like pink melted wax. It came out of her mouth and ears and nostrils, from every opening and orifice.

Still, the hand gripped her head, the fingers luminous and blue.

Susan was reduced to a thrashing anatomical dummy held in place by the seatbelt, a fizzing human seltzer that gurgled and sputtered and oozed, everything she was made of splashing down over the seats and revealing an articulated skeleton darkened by intense heat.

The car was filled with smoke and a mist of blood-steam by that point.

Joe was out of his mind.

He had reached out and touched her several times and had badly scalded his hands. But the burns were nothing compared to the destruction wrought to his mind.

The ghouls outside the car pulled back for reasons unknown and his fingers automatically turned the key and the VW started. He side-swiped a parked car and ripped off part of the front bumper on a big oak tree and then he was driving, occasionally flashing blank looks at the skeleton bouncing around next to him and the perfectly circular hole burned through the glass that was sucking the stink and smoke out into the night.

Gotta get home, he kept thinking. *Gotta get to Megan. Gotta get there. Get there. Get there.*

He drove on, picking up speed, droplets of sweat beading his face. His teeth chattered. His mouth alternately smiled and frowned. His hands were locked on the steering wheel in a death-grip.

And when one of the things stepped into his path, he stomped down on the accelerator. The power was killed before he reached it, but it didn't matter. Even it could not stop the forward momentum of the VW that careened right at it at better than sixty miles-per-hour.

Mass and energy collided.

There was a blinding explosion of blue light as the thing literally broke apart as it was struck. The car, its front end burned, front tires melted, went into a deadly spin and crashed into a house.

Joe came to long enough to realize that his hands were fused to the steering wheel, one melted into the other. But by then, both he and the car were on fire.

27

When Melody got back to her house, Bobby Pistera was standing there with a stunned look on his severely lacerated face. He looked over at her, making gibbering sounds.

"Bobby," she said, her tongue fumbling over the word. "Bobby…oh Bobby."

She didn't know what to say or what to think. Her mind had become a lunatic whirlwind ever since seeing Mrs. Zim burning. It had sprouted wings and wanted to fly right out of her head. She stood there, shaking, making a low gasping sound in her throat, her eyes darting madly.

Bobby looked confused, if anything. As if what had happened to him and what was continuing to happen were just beyond him. Bright rivers of blood had hemorrhaged from his nose and mouth in a brilliant frothing, becoming red creeks and streams that burst their banks and flooded over him. He held out his hands to her in supplication. It looked like they'd been dipped in red paint.

Melody could not find her voice. It had evaporated like a summer pond, filling her throat with black mud and green seepage.

Bobby took two fumbling steps toward her, the strange juicy gibbering sounds he had been making becoming a full-blooded howling that set her hair on end. Blood sprayed from his mouth as he staggered about in the garage in loose circles, bumping into the cabinet and smashing into a rack of tools, leaving a glistening red trail in his wake.

Melody, shocked and helpless, sinking deep in a morass of fear, thought, *what is this? What is this? What's happening to him? What in the hell is happening to him?*

But whatever it was, it was still happening.

He was a crooked, bleeding thing now, crying out in a rasping voice, hands held out like claws, scratching at the air and pawing shovels and rakes from their hooks, casting jars of nails and screws from their shelves to shatter at his feet. His red-stained face was an atrocity, the many cuts having widened into holes that made it look like petrified wood that had been tunneled by generations of termites. His skin looked loose and rubbery like that of a deflated sex doll, his eyes trembling in flayed red sockets that were practically caverns. His mouth opened and closed, fluids gushing down his chin, nothing else coming out now but a phlegmy sort of gurgling.

Melody wanted to help him, to reach out to him, to let him know he was not alone…but she was terrified. The change coming over him reduced her to an oily bag of fear. She could not find her voice or even link together a string of rational thoughts.

White vapor began to hiss from the cracks and holes in him like steam from a leaky pipe. It came out in a swirling mist. His eyes bulged, then exploded from their sockets like splattered grapefruit pulp. His skin was blackening and splitting open and he vomited out a mass of broken crystals and teeth that were stained pink with blood. The smell coming off him was a horrendous, appalling stench of incinerated meat and bone and blood boiled to steam.

The lights flickered, dimmed, then both bulbs overhead popped. No matter, Bobby lit up the entire garage.

It was at this point that Melody hit the floor.

She hadn't even felt it coming. Vertigo just hit her like a bat to the head and her knees folded up and down she went.

But maybe it was for the best because whatever narrow little dusty closet in the back of her mind she had retreated into, she came out now, screaming and ready to fight.

Get away, get away, get away from that damn thing! a voice shouted in her mind.

The monstrosity that had been Bobby Pistera came towards her, smoking and burning, going soft like warm butter, great fleshy curds and sizzling clots of him melting away and dropping to the floor.

"Stay back, Bobby," Melody warned him, her voice breaking with sobs. *"Oh please please please stay back…"*

She realized at that moment that she would never make it to the door before he put his globby, smoldering fingers on her, so she instinctively grabbed the first thing she found which was an old tennis racket that needed restringing.

Bobby kept coming towards her, plopping and oozing, his face hanging by strings like a melting latex mask, revealing a skull beneath that was coldly phosphorescent like an image in an x-ray.

"STAY THE FUCK BACK!" Melody warned him again, this time with rage and ire.

Bobby reached out for her with hands that were blobby and white and seemed to have the same consistency as frying pork chop fat.

Whatever had risen up inside Melody, it was territorial and planned on surviving. As he came towards her, she swung the racket at him, knocking one of his hands aside and freeing it of crawling white meat that sprayed against the wall.

But it barely slowed him.

Whatever was happening to him, it seemed imperative that he put his hands on her. When he tried again, she swung the racket with everything she had, the edge of it splitting his head open like an especially ripe muskmelon, the halves falling free and revealing a toothless skull grinning at her.

She screamed again, tripping over her own feet and narrowly avoiding one of his hands that missed her face by inches.

His skull was hardly the white and gleaming Hollywood variety, but a mask of bone burned yellow and brown, strings of blackened tissue dangling from it like limp worms. There was a pulsating blue glow coming from inside it that made a low humming sound. It lit the garage with a cool blue flickering like an old movie projector.

Melody scrambled out the door on her hands and knees, waiting for his burning hands to find her but they never did. She scrambled through the grass until she was nearly at the house, turning and seeing Bobby standing in the doorway of the garage.

He burst into flames as if he'd been drenched in kerosene.

He stood there, burning and crackling like dry kindling, the garage going up with him, smoke filling the backyard, smoke that was backlit by the raging furnace Bobby now was.

Melody made it around the front of the house and there was a great eruption of force and energy as the garage exploded with fire, sending shards of wood and burning roofing tiles high into the sky.

As flaming debris rained down around her, she walked out into the street as the firestorm spread and her house began to burn.

There was no understanding.

No explaining it.

She could do nothing but watch the flames engulf it and the trees that fronted it. It became a great blazing bonfire whose heat pushed her off farther into the night.

28

Rondleau told him to pull to a stop, so Booth rolled the cruiser to a halt, listening to the constant chatter on the police band.

"What is it?" he asked.

"Another dead one. I want to get a look."

Booth sighed. They'd been in Middleburg a grand total of twenty minutes and they'd already seen over a dozen bodies in the streets—burned ones and others that were nothing but bones that looked like they'd been pecked to death by crows with very hot beaks. He didn't want to see another. In fact, he didn't want any of this. Even though he was a cop, the idea of mixing it up with whatever caused all this was not to his liking.

Rondleau called it in as he'd been calling it in ever since they pulled into town: the burning buildings, the destruction, even the forest fire out on 30 that didn't seem to be heading towards the town but spreading out *from* it.

Now another body.

Shit and shit.

"We'll take a quick look," Rondleau said, releasing the riot gun from its bracket under the dash and gripping it tightly in his hands.

We'll take a look. Booth didn't like that. He would have been only too happy to stay in the cruiser. First off, he was no firefighter; he was a Nebraska state cop. He knew his job and he did it on a daily basis to the best of his abilities. But that didn't involve burning towns. He wasn't trained for it. Secondly, even though he was no coward, there was something terribly wrong here and he had no interest in tangling with whatever it was without some serious backup.

"Come on," Rondleau said, as in *pull your head out of your ass and act like a cop.*

Booth got out, unsnapping the safety catch on his 9mm just because it made him feel better to do so. The smell of smoke was overpowering. A haze of it hung in the streets. Not so far away, he could see the orange glow of fires that were steadily expanding. The heat in the air made him sweat.

Rondleau just stared at him. "You know, you may not like this, Al, but it is our job. Nobody's heard squat out of this town in over five hours now and a lot closer to six. Two sheriff patrols are missing here. The Middleburg force is A.W.O.L. far as we know and Shorty and Pete came in here an hour ago and now they're gone, too."

Shorty and Pete were two State Patrol cops that both Rondleau and Booth knew well, being that they were from the same barracks. They were good friends.

"Maybe you don't care about the rest and I wouldn't put that past you," Rondleau said, "but you sure as hell should care about them. They're cops. They're our friends. Jesus Christ, Shorty loaned you the down payment on your house."

Booth fumbled a cigarette into his mouth and lit it with a badly shaking hand. "Me disappearing, too, ain't gonna bring 'em back."

Man, what a cold and callous thing to say and he knew it. He regretted the words soon as they left his lips.

"You sonofabitch," Rondleau said.

"My nerves are shot, Bill. Something about this place is crawling under my skin. I can't think straight here."

"Well, I can. And first thing I'm thinking is about putting in for a new partner."

"Bill…"

Let him put in, Booth thought. *Let him. Fuck him and fuck this town. None of this is right. A fire might sweep through a town, sure, but it doesn't start in dozens of different locations without an outside agency helping it. And something here, helped it.*

Rondleau turned to the body. He had his flashlight out and he panned it about. Whoever it had been, they were more bones than flesh. A blackened, crispy thing that looked like it had been scraped off the bottom of an oven. It was still smoldering, fingers of smoke rising off it and filling the air with the most revolting, gut-churning sort of smell. It stank like a bale of hair tossed on a bonfire.

Booth had to turn away.

The smell got down inside him and if he hadn't already thrown up what was in his stomach three streets back, he would have voided it right then and right there. This was too much like Fallujah. He had served with the 1st Cavalry Division and Middleburg reminded him of little Iraqi towns hit by the Air Force where they—the 1st—had to go in and make bomb damage assessments. It was so much like it, it gave him the shakes and the sweats. He thought he left that behind ten years ago, but here it was again staring him in the face.

Rondleau examined the body carefully.

Sure, Booth knew, when they got toasted like this they didn't look exactly human any more. This one took such directed heat it was just skeleton really, all broken apart in a zone of black, crispy things that were scattered ten feet.

"Okay," he finally said, "that's enough, Bill. Jesus Christ. Leave it for forensics."

"Just checking it is all. Quit being a pussy."

"You don't know what the fuck you're talking about."

Rondleau got up to tell him that, *yes,* he did...but he saw something in Booth's eyes, something stark and haunted and he knew he had better tone it down before things got ugly.

"Let's go," Booth said.

Rondleau stepped towards the cruiser, a blackened bit of the corpse crunching under his shoe. He heard a funny sort of whirring sound in the distance like the gears of some huge machine whining.

"Hell was that?"

"Let's get out of here before we find out," Booth said.

In the distance, they saw something momentarily in the orange glow of the fire, a sort of pulsating indigo blue light. Then it was gone.

"Blue fire," Booth said.

"Ain't no such thing," Rondleau was quick to point out.

"Then what was it?"

Rondleau swallowed...or tried to...and wiped sweat off his face with his uniform sleeve. "I don't know. Gas or something."

"Or something is right."

They could have argued the obvious for a few more minutes—they'd done that more than once—but they heard footsteps behind them and both swung around. A girl was coming towards them.

She looked like she was about twelve or thirteen, tall and breastless. She looked perfectly ordinary at first glance, save for the relentless machinelike stride that brought her right at them.

"Hey, you," Rondleau said. "You better hold it right there."

But she kept coming and Booth didn't like it at all. He pulled his weapon. He had never killed a kid, not even in the war...at least, not close up like this. But there was ice in his bones suddenly and the flesh at his spine was creeping and he soon saw why.

Rondleau said, "Jesus Christ, put that weapon down!"

But he wasn't putting it down.

The girl kept coming and he was going to put *her* down because she wasn't a girl and he saw it. She stepped on the bones in the street and they crunched beneath her feet. She stepped through them and Booth saw that as her feet touched the pavement there was a sort of hissing sound and little puffs of smoke rose up as if she was burning the street itself. Step. *Ssssst.* Step. *Ssssst.* Step. *Ssssst.* Then she stopped and by then, Rondleau was seeing her and he had the riot gun up.

"No closer," he said, balancing it in one hand, the flashlight in the other. There was fear in his voice and it was cutting deep.

The girl stood there, looking like some badly abused window dummy. Her clothes were blackened strips sucked to her body. Her face and exposed flesh were set with black holes as if she'd been hit by scattershot. The empty sockets of her eyes were shining with quartz-like specks. Smoke started issuing from them, from all those holes. She breathed in and out and when she exhaled, more smoke came out of the cleft of her mouth. Her hair was smoking, too, they saw. It looked like wet hair out in the cold, steam rising from it.

But it wasn't steam.

Smoke was billowing from her now.

Booth lost it and put three rounds straight into her and all that did was open up a few more holes for smoke to ventilate along with a guttering blue light. Heat blew off her in blistering waves. Then her hair lit on fire and within seconds her entire head was burning like a candle.

Rondleau fired a shot from the riot gun in the air, still unable to turn the weapon on a child.

"SHOOT HER!" Booth cried. "GODDAMMIT, SHOOT HER!"

But Rondleau was just out of it. He took two or three steps back, his head slowly shaking from side to side as the girl came for him. The smell of her was horrible, but there was another smell, too, and Booth realized that his partner had just shit his pants.

He grabbed the riot gun and wrestled it away from him.

By then, the flashlight had gone out and the cruiser's headlights were following suit. They dimmed to a dull orange glow and winked out. No matter, the girl lit the night. She came on like a blazing corpse candle, globs of burning fat dropping from her.

Booth didn't waste anymore time: he leveled the riot gun in his shaking hands and pulled the trigger. And what happened after that happened quickly. The buckshot hit the girl and she...exploded. She detonated with force and energy and heat.

He saw it happen.

In fact, it was the very last thing he saw on this mortal plane.

The girl exploded and he saw something like a million blue-hot projectiles streaking at him and then they hit him and Rondleau with devastating force, blasting into them and through them with furnace heat.

And that was it.

The girl had literally vaporized, but what was in her was released like red-hot shrapnel from a bomb. There was a flash of blue-white light and a jumble of cremating bones that had belonged to Booth and Rondleau hit the ground and broke apart.

Other than that, the only sign that they were even there were their images burned right into the paint of the cruiser behind them.

Its tires melted, it settled to the pavement.

Then all was quiet.

29

Tommy McCleesh ran for four blocks after what he'd seen at the police station. He ran past houses and stores he knew very well, a baseball diamond where he'd pitched for Little League back in the day, and the grade school he'd gotten expelled from when he was ten for hitting another boy. But none of it made any impression on him. He needed to flee and flee he did.

Finally, four blocks later, he collapsed against a parked car while a voice in his head asked, *Just what in the hell do you think you're doing?*

But he didn't know.

He really did not know.

His apartment was in the opposite direction and what was there anyway? He was divorced and even his cat had died two months before. There was nothing. And with a despair and bleakness that comes with self-examination, he realized that there really was nothing in his life but driving a fucking cab.

How do you like those bananas? Forty years old, been nowhere, going nowhere, and now even this dirty stinking little town you called home has become some sort of battleground for monsters.

Feeling beaten, the air slowly bleeding out of him, he slid down the car until his ass hit the curb. He sat there like that for a good ten or fifteen minutes, trying to find something inside himself or in his life worth fighting for and coming up fucking blank.

That's because you are a blank. Your cartridge belt has been empty since day one. Other people might find love and friendship, riches and fame, or at least a sad little working class equivalent of the same, but not you. Never you. You were fucked from the moment you came out of your mother and opened your bleary blue eyes.

"Shit," he said under his breath. "Fuck me."

Where all this was coming from, he did not know. He wasn't much on introspection or personal reflection. Maybe that's what had kept his head screwed on tightly all these years. He sat there, thinking, a darkness growing inside of him that he could not feel his way around.

Forty years and you haven't accomplished one constructive, useful thing.

Oh, by Christ, it hurt.

The truth really did hurt.

It was the razor that slit his throat and kept cutting. He felt the gun in his hand and thought about what he could do with it. It would be so easy to end it right here because he wouldn't really be ending anything. It would be more along the lines of putting down a sick dog.

He pulled out a Marlboro and lit it with his Zippo. *At least I won't have to worry about quitting smoking.* He decided that was a plus in a world of minuses. Blowing out a column of smoke, he wondered what the hell was going on in Middleburg and if it was just limited to the town. He finished his cigarette and butted it on the curb.

It was time to get down to business.

If I could have done one good thing, he thought as he studied the gun in the sparse moonlight. *Just one thing.*

Suicide wasn't something that sat on him easily, but he knew it had been on his mind for some time now even if he hadn't actually acknowledged it. This night pushed him that much closer to the edge.

He heard footsteps coming in his direction.

Maybe I won't have to do it myself after all.

But who showed a few seconds later was not one of the things but a woman with a broom. She was dressed in a pink fuzzy bathrobe, flip-flops, and had a Yankees baseball cap on her head. That was incongruous enough, but the broom really sealed it. He couldn't help noticing that one end was badly charred as if she had been stirring coals with it.

She introduced herself as Mona and said she had been through some bad shit.

"I bet you have," Tommy said.

She held up the broom. "I hit one of them in the head, didn't I?" she said as if reading his mind. "Came in the house and I hit him in the head."

"Did it do any good?"

"Nope. You can't stop 'em. They keep coming."

"You're lucky they didn't touch you," Tommy said.

"Touched my husband. Touched Ralph. He burned up. He burned all up."

"Their touch is hot."

Mona nodded sadly. "They don't have eyes."

"No," he said.

"If you're quiet, they can't find you. They can't see you. They need you to make noise."

"The question being," he put to her. "What *are* they?"

"People."

"No, they're not people."

"They touched Ralph and he died. It was that hailstorm. Did you know that? Those people who got caught out in the hail…they were the ones that changed. It's fallout."

"Fallout?"

"From the comet."

The comet? Sure, Issak. It had passed a week ago. It wasn't bright enough to see with the naked eye but the scientists were all excited about it.

"Meteoric debris," the woman told him. "They said we would pass through a zone of meteoric debris for twelve hours, that it would play out by dawn."

Was that it? Was that what had happened?

"Fallout," she said.

"A meteor storm," Tommy corrected her.

She shook her head. "No. *Fallout.* That was the word Ralph's cousin Larry used. Ralph talked to him on the phone. He works for the Jet Propulsion Lab in Pasadena, so he ought to know."

Tommy was more than a little interested now. "What did he say exactly?"

She said Larry had called Ralph the night before and told him to stay indoors tonight because the Earth was passing through a trail of meteoric dust left by Comet Issak that appeared to be charged with some sort of exotic radiation. It would probably amount to nothing and be dispersed like most cosmic dust storms, but you just never knew. If it was to get trapped in an upper air mass and come down as rain—or *hail*—it might be in concentrations that could be dangerous.

"Like fallout," Mona said. "Only not the kind we know, he said."

Tommy didn't like that at all. "So this whole area might be radioactive?"

She shook her head. "No, Larry said if anything happened at all, it would brief...real bad, but brief. By the time it hit the Earth it would evaporate. If you got caught in it—like all those people did—you would absorb it, but if you were inside, you were safe. It would pretty much evaporate."

"Then why weren't people warned?"

"Against what?"

"This dust."

She shrugged. "Larry said it was just a theory. Nobody was interested in it and none of the higher ups at JPL were concerned." She shrugged again. "I gotta go. Ralph is dead...I know he's dead. I ran. Maybe I shouldn't have, but I did. I have to go back."

"Why?" Tommy asked her.

"Brenda. She's my niece. She lives upstairs. I ran off...I got scared...I wasn't thinking. I better go see if she's all right."

Tommy nodded, then thought: *If you want to do something useful, something constructive, something that matters, here's your chance.* He stood up. "Wait a minute. I'll come with you. I have a gun."

"It's worth a try," Mona said.

30

"Abby?" the voice whispered.

Abby stopped, clutching Megan in one arm and holding Denny's hand. She saw a shadow standing there by a hedge, hands on hips. She knew instinctively it wasn't one of the burning people. But who? The voice was recognizable. *David? Was it really David?*

"David?" she said with an exasperation of joy, then remembering that he hadn't called her in a week, her pride got in the way and she simply said, "Hello, David," in a very somber, restrained voice.

"God, am I glad to see you. I was heading over to the Sumners to look for you."

"Why would you be doing that?"

"Because you're my friend," he said, joining her there on the sidewalk. "I was over at your house but no one was there. It was all dark."

Dark? It shouldn't have been dark, she realized then. Mom and dad should have been there. They weren't supposed to be going anywhere. Unless…unless they hadn't gone anywhere but someone or some*thing* had come to visit. Abby shook her head. Oh no, she wasn't going there. She wasn't going to visit that locality unless it was necessary.

"Did you knock?"

"Only about a hundred times."

She felt her heart plummet. She squeezed Denny's hand tighter and cuddled Megan all that much closer. There was no reason to panic. No reason at all. They might have stepped out for a drink or gone out for pizza. Even old Netflix heads like them sometimes did something besides sit on the couch and eat popcorn.

But if they were still alive don't you think they'd be looking for you? You know neither of them would stop until you were safe.

"Are you okay?" David asked.

Yes, he was a teenage boy and a champion of really stupid questions, but this one was an all-time high even for him. "No, I'm not okay. I don't know what's going on."

"Zombies," he said. "At least, that's what I call them. They're everywhere."

Megan was beginning to fuss. "I need to get home with her. Somewhere safe."

"I'll go with you, but to get to your house we have to cross Main Street and those things are everywhere on Main."

"I don't want to go," Denny said.

"It'll be all right," she promised him. Then to David: "What are they? Where did they come from?"

"I don't know, but there's a lot of them."

"We should stay here," Denny said, on the verge of tears.

"No, it's cool," David reassured him. "Don't worry. I won't let them get you."

As they walked, they chatted about this and that in very low tones. Although there were much bigger fish on the griddle tonight, she just had to ask him something. "Why didn't you call me? I waited all week for you to call me." It sounded pathetic and desperate, but she didn't care. Tonight she had a right to sound pathetic and desperate. "Friends call their friends."

She could almost sense how uncomfortable he was. Good, make him squirm, make him twist on the end of the line.

"I don't know," he said, but she could tell from the tone of his voice that he knew very well. "I guess…I don't know. I listened to people maybe."

Oh, there was no *maybe* about it: he had been listening to Todd and she knew it. Todd Benchley. Big dumb macho Todd. That's what she thought and she came right out and said it.

"Yeah."

"And he said something like, *don't give her too much attention, dude. Keep her hungry, keep her wanting. That's how you handle bitches.* Am I right?"

"Yeah."

"You should know better."

"Yeah."

Megan was really starting to fuss. She was getting hungry and she needed a placebo to keep her quiet until they got somewhere safe. Abby turned around so the Gerber backpack was facing David. "Top pouch. Get her Nuk out."

He unzipped the pouch and dug in there. "This?"

Denny giggled. "That's a rattle."

"Oh. How about this?"

"David," Abby said, "that's a stuffed giraffe. A Nuk is a pacifier."

"Oh."

Denny giggled.

David dug it out and handed it to her. It was in a plastic Ziplok bag—always come prepared—and she got it out and stuck it between the baby's lips.

"There, Meggs. Now be quiet until we get where we're going."

Megan beamed up at her in the darkness with her big dark eyes. They gleamed in the night and Abby felt her own eyes grow moist. *I'm sixteen,* she thought. *I'm too young to be in charge like this. I'm too young to be responsible. I can't even remember my locker combo and I failed driver's ed. I'm no one to be responsible for another life.* But it didn't matter what she thought because she *was* responsible and the way Megan looked up at her with complete love and complete faith made her knees feel weak. *She's counting on you to keep her safe. She's counting on you to protect her and so is Denny. What you do in the next few hours will probably be the most important things you'll do in your entire life.* God, the stress of it all. But she'd manage; she'd have to manage.

It would be better with David and she knew it. She already felt a bit safer though she'd never in a million years tell him that. He was a teenage boy and maybe he wasn't real smart, but he was big and he was strong. She would put that to good use as countless generations of women before her had. Brawn had its uses.

Studying the dark, lonely streets ahead, she motioned David over to her, getting her mouth very close to the cup of his ear. "We can't let anything happen to Megan or Denny. We have to keep 'em safe. You know that, right?" He nodded. "Why don't you scout ahead of us a bit and keep an eye out, make sure it's okay. If it's not, you can let me know and I'll hide these two."

"You got it, dude," he said, kissing her on the cheek.

Abby flushed right down to her toes. For a moment there, she got a glimpse of what the future might be like and how good things could be. It gave her a joyful feeling.

"Why are you whispering?" Denny whispered.

"Nothing," she told him. "Watch out for bad guys."

By then, David had stationed himself a good twenty feet or so ahead of them like a soldier walking point. He was really getting into it like a commando slipping through enemy territory, she realized. He'd even found a long, pointy branch that got blown from one of the trees. He was stalking low in a crouch with the stick held out in front of him like a saber.

Good grief, Abby thought.

As they inched ever forward, she again wondered just what was going on. What had turned people, ordinary people like Jim Jensen into monsters. Was it something like in the movies? A mutant virus or a chemical weapon? Something in the water? Something in the air? What happened? Something must have and it must have been extreme. And that got her wondering about mom and dad and Mr. and Mrs. Sumner.

God, this was insane.

Ahead, David stopped. He crept back to them, holding a finger to his lips. He motioned them to follow him into the shadows thrown by a house.

"What is it?" Denny asked.

"Ssshhh," David said.

Out on the sidewalk, Abby saw a long, distorted shadow creeping. She heard the *slip-slap* of what sounded like shuffling bare feet. The shadow grew longer and she grew more tense as she saw what had thrown it. A man. A hunched-over man who moved forward slowly, hands held out before him, fingers wiggling as if he was feeling his way through the darkness. Little arcs of blue light came from him.

Denny began to shake.

Megan's sucking sounds got louder.

He'll hear us, he'll hear us, Abby thought.

He stopped out there on the walk and turned towards the house. They could see the light flickering inside him, the tears and rents in his flesh that let it out. He started moving in their direction with a *hssssst* sort of sound like a sizzling wick. Fingers of smoke came off him, boiling in his wake. He stumbled forward, arms outstretched like the Frankenstein monster off an old black-and-white spook show.

He knows we're here. He either hears us or senses us somehow.

He kept moving in their general direction, shambling off to the left, then the right as if he were casting for their scent. In the end, he always zeroed back in on them.

David pulled away silently.

There was a pile of bricks next to the porch and he picked up one. He crept away from the others, staying in the shadows. He threw the brick a good distance into the yard next door and it crashed into a bird feeder, toppling it over.

The zombie—or whatever he indeed was—moved off in that direction with his Frankensteinian stride. Throwing the brick was the oldest trick in the book, but it worked. The creature followed it to the yard and stopped...then it turned back towards them.

"Shit," David said.

It's attracted to sound but not only to sound, Abby thought. *There's got to be something else that draws it.*

David grabbed another brick. "Here," he said, handing her his phone. "It's got a light on it. You might need it. Head for the backyard. I'll distract him."

Abby took it and David started tossing bricks out into the street. The racket drew the man but never for long. He always turned around and started back in their direction.

David grabbed a couple more bricks and raced across the lawn to draw the creature away from them. He tossed one brick and it intrigued the man but, again, not for long. He threw the second brick right at him. It hit with a thud, driving him back, but not really hurting him. He found his bearings again and started not in David's direction, but in Abby's. David kept trying to distract him, but he always turned in Abby's direction.

She looked down at the phone in her hand.

She thought about her iPhone at the Sumners. One of those things had gotten to it and melted it with its touch. Was that it?

These monsters were drawn towards phones? It was insane…yet the logic would not leave her alone.

She cocked her arm back and threw David's phone out into the street where it clattered across the pavement. At first, it had no effect on the man…then he seized up as if he had taken some serious voltage, then he turned away and sought the phone. Despite being blind, he found it almost instantly and picked it up.

The phone smoked in his hands, running through his fingers in a plastic ooze. He tossed it down and moved away up the street.

Abby clutched Denny tighter to her. He was shivering.

David jogged over. "The phone? It wanted my phone?"

"Seems like it. They went after my phone before."

David sat there by her, thinking as she thought. "Maybe not the phone," he said.

"But something it emits?"

He nodded. "Cells put out EM radiation," he explained. "We studied it in Electronics Two. Not bad radiation but the kind of radiation microwaves make. It's called…um…let me think now…yeah, non-ionizing electromagnetic radiation. An EM field."

"Those things are drawn to the EM. Something about it attracts them and then they seek out whoever's in the vicinity," Abby said.

"Must be."

It wasn't much, but it was something. Anything that would keep them alive was welcome.

Megan spit out her Nuk and sighed, "Googabug," she said.

"Damn straight," David told her.

31

After Mona had showed Tommy McCleesh the remains of her husband—a skeleton that was still simmering with heat—she led him upstairs to check on her niece. The lights were out, something that disturbed him greatly, but she supplied both of them with flashlights.

The walk up the stairs was of short duration, but it seemed to go on and on. They moved carefully and slowly, the steps creaking under their feet and announcing their presence to anyone who might be listening.

At the top, Mona paused, cocking her head and listening. She heard something and Tommy thought he did, too, but what it was neither of them could say. They just stood there in the pooling darkness gripping their flashlights, maybe each secretly hoping that they'd wake up already and the nightmare would end.

But some bad dreams never end.

"You hear something?" Mona asked.

"Thought I did."

She made a *hmmphh* sort of sound that in itself really meant nothing, but he was almost certain he sensed an underlying fear. Mona wasn't right in the head by any stretch of the imagination (as far as he was concerned), but up here she was feeling something and whatever it was, her instincts did not like it.

And I'll just bet she's right on target.

She made another *hmmphh* sound in her throat and set her broom aside as she knocked lightly on the door. "Brenda?" she said. "Brenda? It's me, Aunt Mona. Are you there?"

There was no answer and by that point, Tommy didn't really think there would be. He heard another muted sound from in there and he didn't like it at all. But if Brenda hadn't been out in the hail storm, then there really wasn't too much to worry about.

Unless she's got a visitor in there, he thought.

And that was probably his biggest fear and the one that kept the gun in his hand. There was a smell out on the landing, not terribly strong just terribly wrong. It was a sort of briny, dirty smell of an old well, of things growing in warm darkness that shouldn't grow at all.

"Brenda?" Mona said again.

There was no response so she jiggled the doorknob and found it locked. Ever resourceful, she dug out a set of keys and inserted one into the lock, opening the door. The smell on the landing was worse inside, concentrated and revolting.

"Brenda?" Mona called.

There was only silence as their flashlight beams found a small kitchenette, an old white refrigerator, and a microwave squatting beneath old-fashioned cabinets. They both saw the dirty footprints on the floor, but neither commented on them. Maybe that was for the best.

"Listen," Mona said.

But Tommy already was. That unidentifiable sound they'd heard was clearer inside—a gurgling noise. That's what it was, a gurgling sort of noise like an empty shampoo bottle being rinsed out.

Mona led the way into the living room and they both saw the clothes scattered on the floor. A blazer, a short skirt, one high-heeled shoe. There was probably another around, but they didn't look for it. Again, neither of them commented on the dirty stains on the clothes. They looked like they'd been dragged through an ash bin.

The gurgling came again.

"From in there," Mona said, her flashlight beam piercing the darkness of a doorway and revealing an unmade bed and another cast-off shoe.

Tommy followed Mona in there, his breathing sounding very loud. His hands shook on the flashlight and gun. They heard the gurgling sound and tracked it to a closed door that must have led into the bathroom.

Mona just stood in the doorway of the bedroom as if her feet were glued down. Her face had gone ghost-white and her lower lip trembled. Her body had become some inert mass incapable of movement. She was minutely trembling from head to toe.

"Mona?" Tommy said.

She did not respond, she merely shook her head back and forth slightly. It was shock, he figured. Maybe some sort of delayed reaction to what she had already seen this night. Whatever it was, it reached out and grabbed her, holding her tight. She didn't even seem to be blinking.

Tommy sighed, knowing he was on his own just as he knew the smart thing to do was to get her downstairs. But no one ever said he was smart. He was going to see what was behind that door. Something in him demanded that he do so.

Trying to swallow the desert in his mouth, he went over to the door and put his ear to it. He could hear the gurgling/bubbling sound, but nothing else.

He reached down and turned the knob, pushing the door in. The stink was worse in there, of course, and it came out in a hot, sickening wave like seared chicken guts.

His flashlight beam swept the room, but there was no one waiting in there…only the form in the tub.

"Oh Christ," he said.

There was a woman in there—he could tell that much because he saw one full breast—but other than that, it was hard to say what he was looking at. He only knew it was dead and the stink steaming from the water smelled like boiled marrow and blood. It made him take two uneasy steps backward, dropping the gun and supporting himself against the wall with the flat of his hand. Had there been anything in his stomach it would have come rushing out of him.

He breathed in and out, listening to that ever-present gurgling.

He grabbed the gun and forced himself to stand up and look at what was in the tub. It was nearly full, about four inches from the top, one of those old claw-footed things. The water—which was bubbling like a pot—was brown and fusty, foaming with clots and congealed masses of human grease and curds of tissue which had dissolved from the woman sunk in its depths. She was pitted with dozens of holes and cracked open like an eggshell, a fan of fleshless ribs just breaking the surface, a skeletal hand gripping the edge of the tub, her face melted from the gaping skull beneath into ribbons of meat that floated around her like the tentacles of a jellyfish. The brown slime had overflowed, leaving dark stains down the white porcelain sides of the tub itself.

She was so eaten away, it looked like she had taken a dip in a pool of piranhas or fallen into an acid vat. The gurgling sound was caused by the water sucking in and out of the gaping fissures in her throat. A single eyeball floated like a ping-pong ball.

After staring at her for five or ten seconds, a cold sludge sliding up the back of his throat, Tommy turned away, breathing through his teeth. It was easy enough to imagine what had happened. Brenda—because it had to be her—had gotten caught out in the hail. Her clothes were evidence of that. She had rushed up here, probably in pain because it was burning into her, filled the tub and jumped in.

What happened then was anyone's guess.

Maybe something in the hail combined with something in the water, who the hell knew?

He set the gun on the hamper by the toilet and lit a cigarette to get the smell out of his nose and that awful taste out of his mouth. But more so, he pulled off the butt because he needed the rush of nicotine to get him through what would happen next.

Okay, here's your chance to do something that matters...because that's what you wanted, right? Get Mona out of here. Don't let her see this. Get her downstairs, get some coffee into her, some alcohol, get a blanket on her...whatever the hell you do with people in shock. But, dear God, don't let her see her niece like this.

He stepped into the doorway, pulling off his smoke. "I'm sorry, Mona," he said, "but she's dead. We're going to go back downstairs and sort this out."

That sounded good.

He tossed his cigarette in the sink and reached for his gun— and it was at that precise moment that he heard a wild hysterical scream that ripped right through him. The shock of it was like getting kicked because he thought the dead woman in the tub had done it.

But it wasn't her; it was Mona.

Regardless, the impact of it in that silent tomb of a house, made him stumble back and fall over the toilet, his legs going up in the air and his head hitting the wall. He lost the gun and the flashlight, the latter hitting the floor and rolling about four feet, its beam directed at the tub.

Mona came charging into the bathroom. She saw what was in the water and tossed her light. *"Brenda! Brenda! Brenda!"* she cried in a wounded, frantic voice. *"Oh no...oh no...oh no...BRENDA! BRENDA! BRENNNNNDAAAA!"*

Dazed as he was, Tommy saw what she was going to do and shouted for her to stop, but it was too late. Grief and shock have their own rationale. She reached into the tub and seized the fragmented husk of her niece and she instantly screamed again...but this was not a cry of shock or hysteria but one of absolute mind-numbing agony. Her face was contorted, eyes bulging and peeled open, and that scream just kept coming and coming.

"YAAAAAHHHHHH!" she shrieked in utter, unbelievable pain that peeled her mind raw. *"YAAAAAAAWWWWHHHH!"*

In the flashlight beam, Tommy saw all he needed to see: both arms from the elbow on down were completely skinless. She held them up, water and goo dripping from them, curdled tissue hanging in ribbons. They were raw and steaming, looking much like red shanks of meat that were even then dissolving from the bones beneath.

There was nothing he could do for her.

Whether the fumes got her in those mad seconds after she pulled her arms out of the slop or whether her heart just gave out, he didn't know, but she tottered and fell face-first into the tub, right into the remains of her niece. Water slopped and gurgled, a heavy steam rising up in a fuming cloud as it came to a full boil like a pot. Mona thrashed for a second or two. Brenda had broken apart and Mona came up once, brown slime and fleshy goo hanging down her face that was eaten right down to the skull beneath. One hand gripped the lip of the tub and left four bleeding finger streaks as she sank away into the boiling morass.

Tommy, tears streaking down his face, gagging on the stink and cloying mist of liquefaction, found his gun and flashlight and fled from the room. He tripped over furniture in the living room and bashed against the appliances in the kitchen, then he was half-climbing, half-falling down the stairs.

He didn't stop until he got out into the night and the dry warm wind was blowing over him. Then he went down on his knees, nearly out of his mind, knowing full well that the road to hell was most certainly paved with good intentions.

32

After State Patrolmen Rondleau and Booth did not report in for thirty minutes—which brought the number of missing cops to nearly twenty—the order was cut and the Nebraska National Guard's 1047th Transportation Company rolled towards Middleburg. Led by tactical vans of the Nebraska State Patrol and troopers in full riot gear, they were ordered to set up roadblocks to stop any incoming traffic and secure a safe perimeter.

Once said perimeter was organized, Guard and police units would begin moving into the town to evacuate survivors and provide them with emergency medical care and/or security. At the same time, incident management teams were choppered in and firefighting crews would establish zones around the town.

By that point, one of the major responsibilities of both the Guard and police would be to keep out the curious and the media. Already, stories were flying across the internet concerning everything from UFOs to bioterrorism. Nobody knew anything so the more imaginative types were more than happy to fill in the blanks.

By three a.m., there were 150 men closing in on Middleburg and by dawn it would be twice that and by noon of the next day, there would be upwards of a thousand.

There had been three reconnaissance flights over the town by that point and all had reported the same things—fires burning out of control in various locations, but other than that no overt signs of civil disturbance in the streets. Those individuals that were spotted from above were usually alone or in pairs. There were no roving mobs that could be seen. Some areas of the town were blacked out and many of those that were still lit up, appeared to be eerily silent.

The bottom line was that no one had any idea what was really going on down there. Telecommunications were down, even landlines interrupted, and the only thing that could cause that was purposeful intervention by persons or persons unknown or by directed electromagnetic/microwave interference of the sort no one even wanted to contemplate.

33

For the longest time, Melody wandered with no set direction. What she had seen snapped something in her, opening a deep and bleeding laceration in her mind that she could not close. So, in shock and nearly mindless, she walked and walked, a tall woman in a bathrobe, her long hair plastered to her sooty face, a tennis racket in one hand.

C'mon.

C'mon, snap out of it already.

The voice was inside her head and at first, its words meant nothing to her, but gradually they began to make sense and the more sense they made, the more she was drawn out of herself. She blinked. She swallowed. She shook. And finally, she let out a little high, piercing shriek.

Then she stood there, remembering and wishing she couldn't. The wheels turning in her brain once again, she realized that she was standing out there in a bathrobe, carrying a tennis racket. She must have looked like a crazy person.

Okay, that's better. Now you're getting your shit together. Think and keep thinking.

Which was good advice because coming down the sidewalk, probably attracted by her shriek, were two...*things.* They looked vaguely like people at this distance but she could see very well from the flickering energy bursting from them that they were not people.

Her entire body came alive with pure animal panic then. And just in time. Not running, not just yet, she walked very quickly into a yard and cut between two houses. She saw another thing standing on the patio of a dark house. It heard her and moved in her direction. Another came from the alley.

Melody responded in kind.

Panic breaking loose in her and making her heart drum, the breath rasp in her lungs, and her head pound relentlessly, she climbed over some hedges and ran up a hill, then took a set of steps that led back down to the alley.

It was dark down there and she ran right into the back end of a parked car, knocked flat and breathless. She scrambled to her feet, swinging the tennis racket around in the darkness and encountering absolutely nothing.

Okay, keep going! You're not safe yet. Don't just stand here like a bimbo in a horror movie, move your ass. Grab some pavement and put it to use!

She started moving again.

But where was she going?

What place in this damn town was really safe now?

She paused at the mouth of the alley, thinking, reasoning. It was as she did so that she heard a sound that disturbed her even more than the things themselves—it was a distant whirring sound that reminded her very much of a power saw, but bigger, louder, thicker somehow.

Coming down the street were a pack of the things, casting about for something to latch onto. She doubled back and slipped through a gate into a backyard enclosed by a high fence. The house before her was tall and dark. Those to either side were nearly touching it. She saw from the flashes of light that she was being hunted down. The sky in the distance was orange from fires and she could smell charred wood.

She ran up to the house and thankfully, the patio door was open. Why not? Whoever locked their doors in Middleburg?

She stepped into the darkness, considered searching for a light but decided against it. She closed the patio door and peered out into the night. Yes, those things were still in the alley. No. *Shit.* One of them was standing the backyard. It looked like a teenage girl. She stood there staring at the house with the black holes of her eyes. Tendrils of smoke rose from her.

Melody threw the lock and felt her way around in the darkness. She bumped into something which her hand told her was a table. She found the flat face of a refrigerator, then a stove. She moved on, her night vision getting a little better. Here was a dining room which led into a living room. This was good. Now out into a hallway. She could see moonlight coming in through a window. Good. Here was the front door in a well of shadows.

Excellent.

She found the knob. It was locked. She found the catch and unlocked it. She started opening it and realized that she wasn't alone. There was a shape standing in the corner just to the right of the door and she gasped. The shape made a sizzling sound and a soft blue glow pulsed from it.

Fuck!

Melody threw the door open, smashing it into the shape and fighting forward. There was a screen door and she went right through it, tearing out the screen and falling to the porch, banging her knee but good. She crawled down the steps and into the grass, panting.

She'd lost her tennis racket now but she figured she could live without it. Hugging a tree and scoping out the night, she heard that whirring sound again. It sounded louder this time, definitely much closer.

What in the hell is that?

It came and went and each time it did, she could feel a steady sort of vibration under her feet that made her toes actually tingle. It wasn't a natural sound and she knew it. It couldn't possibly be good and what scared her the most was that her flight had taken her closer to it.

She looked behind her.

That shape in the house wasn't coming after her, at least not yet.

Time to move.

Time to get somewhere.

Time to find a good place to hide before that awful whirring got any closer because she knew without a doubt that it most surely would.

She stepped out in the street and saw the lights of a vehicle approaching. She ran out there and flagged it down. It was a huge, lumbering truck and she saw it was a fire truck. Two men jumped off and approached her with what looked like rifles in their hands. But as they got closer, she could see that they were actually gun assemblies connected by hoses to tanks on their backs.

"She's got eyes, she's okay," one of the men said, directing a powerful halogen beam in her face.

Then hands grabbed her and she was hoisted up into the roomy cab.

"I imagine you got a story to tell," one of them said.

34

By the time Abby and the others made it out to the sidewalk again and had gotten less than a block, hoping to make the last leg of the journey to her parent's house, there were people in the streets, dozens of them.

But, of course, they weren't people at all.

They were things that had come out of the night, mutant creatures blazing in their own supercharged auras. Things attracted by sounds and the EM fields produced by cell phones. Things that needed badly to touch any living creatures they found.

The evidence was everywhere.

There were bones scattered on the walks, in the street, in yards. Most of them were human but many were of animals, probably dogs and cats. And as horrendous as all that was, it was hardly the worst thing because that was the creatures themselves.

Abby and Megan, David and Denny were crouched in the bushes and none of them seemed to know what to do.

What could they do?

Really, what could they do?

You're never going to make it home, Abby told herself. *The idea is ridiculous. There's too many of them, just too many.*

They seemed to be coming from the north side of town. Maybe, whatever had happened to them, it had happened over there or been much more severe over there. When she looked northward, there was no disguising the fact that there was a sort of pulsating blue glow coming from that direction.

"It must be coming from them," David said. "There must be a lot of them over there."

Which made perfect sense, Abby decided. It looked like a nuke had been set off over there or a UFO had crashed or something.

Or something.

She watched the creatures out in the streets marching around with no set direction in mind. Some only flickered a bit now and again, but others were definitely glowing more than not now.

When they walked, they left a weird afterglow of charged particles behind them.

"Here's what we have to do," David said. "We have to go back, cut around and try another street. There's got to be a way around them."

"What if there's not?" Denny asked.

"There will be."

Abby wished she could share his optimism, but it seemed to her that things were getting very bleak. There wasn't a lot of hope before, but now there was definitely none. She had hoped, maybe, in the back of her mind that there might be a dozen or so of those things in the streets but now she knew the problem was much, much worse than that.

No matter, they had to move.

Gripping Denny's hand and cuddling Megan to her—who was sucking very loudly on her Nuk by that point and needing something more and soon—they followed David back the way they had come. At the corner, he led them across the street to where there were no things waiting around. So far, so good.

And it was then they heard a man shouting.

"Got Rich and George and little Frank!" he cried into the night, apparently out of his head. *"Then they got Kathy and Louise and even the twins! Even the twins, I say!"*

Abby stood there on the sidewalk in the warm wind. David stood with her. What now? What was this now?

"Didn't stop there!" yelled the crazy man. *"Went house to house like...like...like ghouls and vampires and dead things that wouldn't lay down! Knocking on doors! Bang-bang-bang! You home, Mrs. Micheaud? How about you, Mr. Peel? Mind if I stop for a time, Miss Baroni? Hee-hee-hee, haw-haw-haw! Bang-bang-bang!"*

Then they saw a figure coming down the avenue. He was a guy maybe in his thirties, shirtless, pumping a rake in the air like he was the leader of the band. He stomped his feet and shouted and spun in circles right up the middle of the street, just completely off his nut.

"Hey, hey, hey! What do you say!" he cried. *"They're coming and you can't stop 'em! What's that, Mr. Jones? You got a gun?*

Hoo-ha! Guns don't work, you fucking shiteater! You might as well throw fucking macaroni at 'em! What say, Mrs. Wiggins? Got yourself a Samurai sword your daddy took off a dead Jap on Tarawa? Well, good gracious and grab-ass! Bow down before Lord Toyota and Sir Mitsubishi and Lady Nintendo, you silly twat! You can't slice 'em, dice 'em, peel 'em or julienne 'em! They'll burn you up like a match head! What you think this is? Some half-ass dumb shit zombie show where you Samurai their asses with swords? Ha-ha! Ha-ha! Ha-ha-ha-ha-ha!"

That was enough.

It was getting not only scary but freaky. David led Abby and the kids into a yard behind a fence, but apparently they didn't move fast enough because here came crazy man with his crazy rake which was the symbol of office in Whacko-land.

"I see ya! You brats can't hide from me!" he ran in their direction and shook the rake at them, but got no closer. *"Over here! Lookee over here, you zombies! We got ourselves some nice farm fresh young meat you can burn up! Right here! Right here! Right here!"*

David, still carrying his pointy stick, got the others behind him. "Get away from us! If you come any closer, I'll kick the shit outta you!"

The crazy man found that amusing because he danced in circles doing a lunatic Irish jig. *"Hoo-weeee! C'mon, you deadheads, this boy is spicy and seasoned! Come and get it! Come and get it! Come and get it!"*

Both Denny and Megan were crying and Abby didn't feel she was too far away herself because the zombies *were* coming. Oh yes, they were coming in force, flickering and sputtering, eyeholes lit with starfire, burning up from the inside out but not so soon that they couldn't add a few more victims to the ever growing list this night.

The crazy man was dancing and panting, his chin wet with drool. *"You got it! You got! Step right up, children! Step right up to the buffet! We got your roasty, toasty, fresh and crunchy kid right here! RIIIIIYYYYYYGHT HERE! GET 'EM! GET 'EM! WEINIE ROAST! WEINIE ROAST! ROOOOOOOAAAASSSSST! YUM! YUM! YUMMMMMMMM—"*

He never finished that because a man stepped from behind a tree and walked right up to him and said, "Shut the fuck up," and punched him square in the face, dropping him sobbing into the avenue. Whoever the guy was, he came over to Abby and the others. "You kids all right? Okay, c'mon, we better get inside as quick as we can. Those damn things are massing everywhere."

He had no sooner spoken those words than two of them came out of the darkness, snapping and popping and throwing out a thick acrid smoke. By then, the crazy man had found his feet and that was the worst thing he could have done.

They seized him from both sides and he screamed as their fingers sizzled right into his flesh like red-hot pokers. He jerked and fought, his hair blazing like straw, his eyes boiling in their sockets like five-minute eggs and bursting with the bubbling yolks of his optic nerves. About the time he split open with a sound like a cracked walnut, and his insides gushed from him like hot wax, Abby and the others and their new friend were on the move.

"Hurry!" he said.

35

Third Platoon of the 1047th was one of the first units to enter Middleburg. They made it approximately three blocks into the town when a group of five people came running up the street to them, shouting.

"THEY'RE COMING!" one of them yelled. "THEY'RE RIGHT BEHIND US!"

The soldiers got the people away behind a barrier for safety and then a group of five guardsmen moved forward with tactical lights bolted to their M4 rifles. At first, they saw nothing. There was only the town standing empty as a coffin around them. Then—

A group of seven individuals closed in on them and they could see quite plainly in the beams of their lights that there was something desperately wrong with them.

Squad leader Sergeant Kolan got on the bullhorn immediately. "STOP! I WANT YOU PEOPLE TO STOP RIGHT THERE FOR YOUR SAFETY AND OUR OWN! IF YOU DO NOT, WE WILL BE FORCED TO RESPOND!"

Whether the seven individuals heard him or even understood what he was saying was uncertain because they kept coming forward, each of them sizzling and throwing off clouds of churning smoke like demons breaking through the gates of hell.

Kolan did not hesitate and neither did his men.

They opened up, firing three-round volleys into the individuals that seemed to do nothing more but further ventilate them so that more smoke blew out of them until it filled the streets in a fuming haze.

Two men broke and ran and reinforcements charged forward. Three others—Kolan included—stood their ground, emptying their magazines into their attackers.

But by then it was far too late.

The attackers had closed with the soldiers and by then they were burning hot and what came next made the reinforcements skid in their tracks. The individuals—like burning corpses by that point—opened their puckered oval mouths and exhaled a directed stream of fire at the soldiers which engulfed them instantly.

A survivor of Third Platoon would later say, "It was like Godzilla, you know? They was breathing fucking fire."

The three members of Third Platoon burned as did the overhang of a nearby house. One of them—Kolan again—managed to crawl from the blaze like a heap of burning, oily rags. He didn't make it much further than three or four feet before collapsing.

And then to the absolute horror of the Third, the seven individuals walked right through the cordon of flames, all of them on fire and heading straight towards the soldiers who wasted no more time. They withdrew to a safer location and lobbed grenades at their attackers who were less than twenty-five feet from them by that point.

It was the worst thing they could have done.

The grenades found their marks, going up in a series of booming concussions and the individuals exploded with them, releasing a superhot emission of charged particles that roasted the remainder of Third Platoon in their own skins and rendered their vehicles to blackened, pitted heaps.

36

As the fire truck moved down the street, something inside Melody finally opened up and she started talking. What amazed her was that once she started, she couldn't seem to stop. She poured out her guts to the four members of the Keith County Volunteer Fire Department—Stone, Taiden, Quigg, and Janessen—who listened without interrupting her until she just wound herself down. "…and I ran and I kept running…but I kept seeing them everywhere—but, God, what the hell are they? Like zombies? Like monsters? I mean, *what the hell are they?* Things like them can't be…they can't take over a whole fucking town! Why isn't something being done? Why isn't this situation being handled? Doesn't anybody give a shit? *Why isn't something being done?"*

"Something is being done," Janessen told her. "But it's gonna take time. For now, we're going to get you out of here."

"But they won't let you."

He smiled. "Oh, they'll try to stop us, but we know how to handle them so don't worry."

"We're pros," Quigg said.

Taiden and Stone up front just laughed.

How can they laugh? How can they be so calm? Melody wondered. She sat there, hugging herself. She had a fire helmet on now and a heavy fire jacket. She realized she must have looked quite a sight in that gear with her bathrobe on underneath. The absurdity of it made her laugh.

"You all right?" Janessen asked.

"Just thinking I must look quite the fright," she said.

He laughed now. "I think under the circumstances you look pretty good."

"Real good," Stone said.

"Ignore him," Quigg said. "He's a pervert."

"You say that like it's a bad thing," Stone said.

They all had a little chuckle over that but it didn't last long as they passed through a neighborhood where every house was burning. They cut down an avenue and right away the headlights of the fire truck began to dim.

"Okay, kill it," Janessen said.

"They're coming," Melody gasped, the fear like a spike inside her.

Stone rolled the truck to a stop and killed the lights and engine. He explained that the firestarters out there—as he called them—had some kind of energy field that disrupted electrical systems. It was better to shut the vehicle off rather than drain the battery.

Quigg and Taiden stepped outside with those tanks strapped to their backs. Right away, two of the firestarters approached them, both arcing in some kind of electric blue web. They aimed the gun assemblies in their hands at them and hosed them down with something like water, only thicker and foaming.

Both firestarters dropped, encased in it.

Stone tried the lights, but there was still interference.

"We better clear this area or we're going nowhere," Janessen said.

They trooped out and Melody went with them. The idea of being alone again was just too much for her to bear.

She looked around in the moonlight at the ravaged town that she'd lived in for the past seven years since moving from North Platte. Not everything was burning, of course, but a lot of it was. The fire had already rushed through much of the neighborhood they were in. Windows were shattered, storefronts blackened, many structures collapsed into pyres that were still burning. The air was hot and thick with a fog of smoke.

Against a brick wall, she saw the darkened images of three people that looked like they were rendered in charcoal. That was all that remained of them. There weren't even any bones around.

"What kind of heat can do that?" she asked Quigg, but he just shook his head.

"Back," Taiden said. "We got contact."

Melody got well behind the four of them.

She saw a half-dozen firestarters coming at them with their slow, meandering funeral march sort of pace. They were sizzling and smoking, throwing out plumes of spiraling black ash. Their faces were white enamel punched with numerous black and bloodless holes. The closer they got, the more heat they radiated. They were haunted, eyeless things that lit up now like cigarettes, their heads igniting like burning suns. They held out blazing fingers.

Melody was trembling, trying to keep quiet but a whimpering made it out. She could taste the salt-sweat on her lips.

"Come and get it," Stone said.

The firestarters needed no further urging.

They stepped forward and Melody saw them open their ragged mouths. She saw the flickering blue glow coming from the channels of their throats. Flames were gathering in there, ready to be put to use.

They never got the chance.

The firemen hosed them down. They all carried the tanks on their backs and whatever was in them gushed out and inundated the firestarters.

It stopped them.

Stopped them dead.

Melody saw it happen. They were like burning cigarettes dropped into puddles. They went out with a sort of *hsssst* kind of sound. Two of them stumbled forward and pitched over face-first, shattering like sculptures of dry clay on the pavement. Broken up like that, scattered and disjointed, they didn't even look like anything that could possibly have lived.

The others followed suit and hit the ground.

Whatever was in the tanks simply extinguished them. It left a sort of sweet, not unpleasant odor in the air that reminded her of green apples.

"What is that stuff?" she asked when Janessen came over to her.

He wiped soot from his face. "It's water basically that's mixed with a liquid polymer called FireIce. That's the brand name. It creates a gel that cools anything off instantly. Fire can't burn when it's hit with this stuff. If I covered your garage in FireIce, even napalm wouldn't ignite it. It couldn't."

"Do you have a lot of it?"

"Enough to cut us a path right out of this town and enough to drop hundreds of firestarters. They can't fight against this stuff."

Melody just stood there, watching the firemen with dirty jackets, faces blackened by ash and smoke. She realized then and there that ever since she was a little girl she had been looking for heroes, knights on white horses and all that romantic gobbledegook that fills a child's head. And here she was, an adult woman, and she had really found some and, by God, she was not about to let them get away.

37

Their new friend's name was Tommy and Abby and the others blindly followed him, very happy to let an adult be in charge of them. Something Abby would never have admitted on any ordinary day.

He moved out ahead of them with David while she hung back with Megan and Denny. It was pretty much the way they had been moving before only now Tommy was at the wheel doing the steering. They passed through neighborhoods that were burning, moving hesitantly through clouds of drifting smoke and she was never sure if he was leading them out of it or further into it.

You just have to trust. That's all you can do. He acts like he knows what he's doing so you'll simply have to trust that he does, she thought.

He was against them moving in the direction of her parents' house. He said things were worse over there. He just wanted to find somewhere safe where they could rest for a time, then they'd make their way out of town.

They came across things she would never forget, the sort of shocking images that would forever haunt her subconscious, showing up in nightmares for the rest of her life. It wasn't just the bones scattered in the streets, but groups of people laying in yards that looked as if they'd been flash-fried. They were not skeletons and not corpses exactly, but crumbling things somewhere in-between. Trees were burning and church steeples lit like candles. Rooftops were set ablaze along with telephone poles.

That was something that didn't make a lot of sense. It was almost like the real heat was coming from above.

The wind stank of burning bodies and bonfires and searing smoke.

When she looked north, she saw that curious blue glowing, but to the east and west it was orange light, the light of fires. The only good thing was that she was starting to hear sirens and fifteen minutes before she had heard the sound of a helicopter to the south.

Ahead, Tommy stopped and Denny stopped with him.

"Quick!" he cried. "There's more fire-eaters coming!"

Abby could see that coruscating blue light flickering and flashing against the clouds of smoke hanging overhead.

Megan was getting fussy.

Not now, baby, not now.

38

The town was haunted by hot winds and blowing irradiated dust, ghosts from kilns and smelting ovens that breathed out hot red ashes and moved in wakes of cremated flesh and bone. It was a great coal-black skeleton shattered in a tomb with smoldering cinders in its eye sockets and scratching black sticks for fingers. Its children—eyeless, mindless, marrow hot as plutonium—were born in forest fires and crematory pits, moving in columns of hot steam and searing black pitch, owning the night and filling minds with terrible fevers and the air was a congested, rancid heat.

Like the melting core of a reactor, the town kept burning right down to its bones that snapped and popped in the great incinerator of Middleburg.

39

The fire truck, once Stone got it running again, rolled on another four blocks before concentrations of the firestarters made the lights dim and the engine catch. They were out on foot again, making enough noise to draw everyone of those goddamn things down on them.

And they came.

They moved forward, hot and seething and the firemen hosed them down with foaming clots of FireIce that clipped their wicks and cooled them off. They blackened and cracked open, breaking apart in the streets. But there were always more.

In the distance, Melody could hear people screaming and there was no help for them. No protection, really, from the things that knocked on their doors and burned them up in their beds and lit their houses aflame. Even after the screams ended, they did not really end. They echoed inside her skull. They lived inside her, haunting her bones like ghosts of the long dead in a ruined cathedral.

Hearing a strange snapping and popping like cedar knots in a fireplace, a fresh wave of heat blew in from the west and made sweat run down her face in warm rivers. She climbed up on the step of the truck and in the distance she saw treetops bursting into flame but she could not see what had caused it.

But that knowledge was coming.

She knew it would be hers because it was bearing down on her and she could feel the rumble of its approach as it got closer and closer.

The firemen kept hosing down the firestarters and she couldn't seem to remember just how many they had put down, but the longer they were at it and the more tanks of FireIce gel that they emptied, the quieter they became. Gone was the good cheer and brotherhood. It was replaced by a sullen brooding and a fear that whitened the eyes in their sooty faces.

You can't put out every fire in hell, she thought. *Maybe you can extinguish hell's perimeter, but its hot beating heart will blaze on and on.*

When it seemed Janessen and the others simply couldn't go on, the firestarters swarmed out like locusts eager to strip fields and they had no choice but to keep fighting until they were standing knee-deep in the retarding gel.

Then came revelation.

What she dreaded and maybe had felt deep in her heart ever since hearing that inexplicable whirring sound, arrived.

It arrived with the firestarters.

A dozen of them blocked their escape route.

They waited at the intersection like scarecrows in a cornfield, withered and steaming things, waiting with a patience and a diabolic intent that was completely inhuman at its dark roots.

The firemen recharged their canisters of FireIce and started moving out to greet the newcomers.

And it was at that moment that something inside Melody went electric and she started shouting. "NO! NO! GET BACK! SOMETHING'S GOING TO HAPPEN! GET BACK! *PLEASE!*"

But they marched ever forward like soldiers charging into the bloody teeth of the enemy and not her screaming or crying out did a damn bit of good to slow their inevitable progress. She was some clichéd damsel-in-distress watching the good knights of her kingdom wading in at the fiery mouth of an immense dragon.

There was nothing she could do to help them.

There was no way to make them understand the WARNING inside her or the THREAT of it, that something very much like manic survival instinct within her had gone from potential to kinetic. She could not understand it anymore than she could truly put a name to it. But it was there. It was vast and it owned her. It rooted her to the spot like a centuried oak and all she could do was cry out in a broken, feeble voice that bounced out into the night and returned to her unanswered and unheeded.

And though she was not a religious person, something in her cried out: *Oh God, oh God, call them back before it's too late! Let them feel what I'm feeling! Let them know that the warning shadows are gathering!*

Then...the firemen stopped.

They were less than thirty feet from the firestarters. They caught a hint of something. Whatever it was, it was enough to stay them if only momentarily until their testosterone ordered them forward again.

The heat radiating from the firestarters spiked.

Even where Melody was, back near the truck, she could feel it. It was burning against her skin like a bright August sun at the beach. The firestarters were trembling with it. And from them came an unearthly sort of vibration that nearly knocked them off their feet. It increased as did a low electronic humming they put out.

The fireman were pushed back and then back again by the heat.

Melody clung to the truck, the vibrations coming up through her feet and making her bones rattle and the fillings in her teeth feel like they were going to shake themselves loose. Then…then the firestarters began to crisp and blacken without ever truly catching on fire. That blue glow inside them—that she had once acquainted with a pilot light in a gas furnace—grew brighter and their flesh cracked open with dozens of intersecting hairline fractures and the light spilled out of them like blood, pulsing and blinding. She saw something like a wire-thin blue-white tendril erupt from one of the cracks. It threaded its way out until she saw that it was branching like a bolt of lightning or, and more precisely, like the synapse of a brain cell. Then another came out and another and another. Two of them grew like spreading rootlets from one of the firestarters' eyes, then another from its mouth until it looked like it was infested by some parasitic weed…but one that was electric blue-white and pulsating, ever pulsating.

The firestarter seized up.

It cracked open like a roasted husk of corn and she saw something huge, oblong, and globular rise from the remains. It was like an immense, grotesque eyeball in shape with a branching synaptic network of tendrils fanning out around it. The orb was blazing blue-white, the size of one of those giant beach balls, and she had to shade her eyes to look at it.

The other firestarters split open to birth similar orbs that drifted about, leaving trails of luminous dust in their wakes.

Was she seeing this?

Was she, by God, really seeing this?

Something in her mind seemed to go gibbering and mad at the sight of those things. They threw off such an intense incandescence that she could almost feel her retinas frying if she tried to look directly at them. They were like iridescent jewels of primary cosmic creation, white-hot ejecta left over from the Big Bang itself.

And the heat coming off them…it made her feel like her skin was sweating off in a greasy sheet. As she stumbled back, her face and legs felt horribly—and painfully—sunburned as if she was being turned on a spit over glowing red coals. Only the heavy fire-retardant yellow Nomex jacket kept her body from feeling the same.

She backed away until she felt moderately cooler.

Still shading her eyes, she could see the things moving with a slow weightlessness twenty feet off the ground, their tendrils waving about them lazily as if they were underwater or in some fluid medium that was thicker than air and with a greater atmospheric pressure.

One of them drifted towards a row of elm trees fronting a boulevard and they burst into flame one after the other. Another did the same at a row of houses, bathing them in a brilliant white light right before they exploded into flame.

Yet another of them was coming right up the street. One of the firefighters broke and ran, the others simply overcome by the heat. They went up in flames as if they had been doused in gasoline…the intensity of the orb's heat cooking them into burning fragments that were sucked up into its mass, creating a rippling across its surface as they were assimilated.

It was coming for her next.

Melody ran stumbling down the street, shedding her heavy coat and helmet. She looked back once and the orb was twenty feet from the fire truck. Its tires melted and it dropped to the street, windows blackening and falling apart, paint running like blood and then it erupted in a rolling ball of fire.

Then she was running.

And running.

And running.

40

Reg Jannessen jogged away in his heavy jacket, fire pants, and boots. His face was blistered and suppurating, his left eyelids fused together. The orb was coming for him and he could feel its approaching heat. He could outrun it; it was slow…but it would keep coming and coming. He had seen Stone and Taiden and Quigg reduced to flaming ragdolls that were eroded into fiery bits that the thing pulled into itself.

He kept running. Moving forward, he stumbled in his boots, but knew he did not have the time to stop and take them off. That thing would bake him if he did.

The heat was being directed at him in oscillating waves. It was like being in a convection oven. Bushes near to him withered and blazed up with flames. Paint blistered on houses. Fences started on fire.

But he had to keep going.

He had to distance himself from it.

I'm not alone, not alone, not alone, he thought as he saw people—real people—running from houses like stampeding animals to avoid the thing and its heat.

The living inferno pushed ever forward with that whirring sound that set his nerves on edge. That, combined with the pain he was in, made it hard to stay on his feet. He stumbled. He fumbled. He tripped over a bird feeder and smashed into a porch.

Each time he got up.

Each time he kept moving.

Then he felt a wave of searing heat strike him. He was lifted in the air and thrown right into a brick wall. Bleeding, broken, senseless, he tried to climb up and over it and, to his credit, he nearly made it. But as he scrambled over the top, he ignited in a flaming plume and dropped to the yellowed grass a corpse that was black and fissured.

41

First Platoon's original objective, of course, was to evacuate survivors of Middleburg and get them out to the safe zone beyond the town's boundaries. But that quickly went to shit when they lost four men to the natives—as they were being called—and had to re-think exactly what it was they were doing and what their primary mission was.

Now that the fire was blazing away out of control behind them, there was no possibility of retreat, so Platoon Leader Lieutenant Chavers decided the best thing to do was to make for the west side where they'd could (hopefully) link up with Second Platoon.

But even that wasn't looking so good now.

Middleburg had become a maze in the fire. There was no direct path in any direction. Burning neighborhoods and smoke-filled streets meant starting this way, then turning that way, cutting over two blocks and then getting back in the direction you had started from. But with the general confusion, it wasn't always so easy.

Chavers moved his little convoy of two Hummers and one half-ton truck forward carefully. The boys were getting edgy, but he didn't dare rush them into a situation they weren't prepared to handle. Too much was at stake.

Ahead, the flames fanned out and another block of homes went up, two tall and narrow Victorian monstrosities on the corner rising up like pillars of fire.

The lead element of the platoon was too close and several men came running down the street, their uniforms on fire. They were put out quick enough, but another avenue was closed to them.

Chavers ordered everyone to cut down an alley to the left which they did in no little hurry. The vehicles moved on and he could feel the tension building because the men were worrying that they were going to get sandwiched in by the fire and never make it out.

All communications were down and Chavers didn't like that. He couldn't even call in for a chopper to evac his people out if it came down to it. It was all on him now and he could very much feel that his boys were losing faith in him.

"Lieutenant!" someone called. "It's following us!"

It was inconceivable, but a line of fire was cutting through the neighborhood directly at them. Fire didn't act that way. Not unless it was directed. Panic was setting in and the vehicles were trying to overtake each other in their mad flight as men on foot ran in all directions and Chavers shouted at them over the bullhorn.

He saw one of the Hummers smash into a parked car and the men jump out. But it was no good. He saw them burst into flame one after the other, then the Hummer itself went up. The air was filled with a smell like frying bacon.

Oh Jesus...those men...those poor fucking men...

But Chavers didn't spend too much time mourning them because his own driver was pouring it on, trying to get them out of there. Everything was in chaos and there was no way Chavers was going to reign his boys in. Not now. Not with the thing that came drifting through a curtain of fire, bearing right down on them.

42

Melody stopped in her mad flight when she heard vehicles heading in her direction. Not just vehicles but men on foot. Voices crying out. Shouting to one another. Holding onto a tree, she saw a Hummer come racing down the street followed by another truck, a group of men in what looked like full battle gear trying to catch up with them.

The National Guard.

It had to be the National Guard.

But they were heading right into the path of the orb.

She ran out there, trying to flag down the vehicles but the Hummer went right past her and the truck nearly ran her right over.

"WAIT!" she called to the men. "WAIT! YOU CAN'T GO THAT WAY!"

One of the soldiers knocked her out of the way and then another knocked her right down and then they were moving towards the orb.

There was nothing she could do.

Bruised and battered, she pulled herself out of the street and saw the orb coming. The vehicles skidded to a halt and the truck smashed into the Hummer. The orb moved in their direction, humming like a transformer, whirring like a saw, glowing like the eye of cat. The vehicles exploded into flame like they were hit with napalm, a huge gushing corridor of fire spread across the street. The soldiers tried to escape and went up like dry scarecrows as that cold blue-white glow bathed them. She saw a couple of soldiers that were on fire still running. They made it maybe ten feet before they were pulled off their feet by the suction of the orb and atomized into burning cinders that were absorbed by it.

The dead, cremated men on the ground suffered the same fate. And as the orb ingested them, it grew larger. She saw it. Before, it had been the size of one of those ridiculously large beach balls and now it had to be thirty feet in circumference. Arcs of blue electricity forked from its waving tendrils, hitting trees and houses and making them burn.

And still the orb came on, drifting forward, flames erupting in its path.

43

Tommy chose the house pretty much at random, but once they got in there he knew he had made the right choice. The house was brick. That was something. He knew the fire-eaters could burn through wood—he'd seen that during his wild flight from Mona's when they'd followed him into a house and come right through the walls—but he didn't think they'd get through brick.

At least, he hoped not.

There were still windows but there was nothing he could do about that. His mind still reeling from everything he'd seen that night, he forced himself to mellow by degrees. He'd tried to do the right thing with Mona, but that situation had rapidly cycled out of control. Now here he was with Abby and David, baby Megan and little Denny. Here was something worth fighting for. Here was a good fight if only he could figure out how to wage it.

One good thing, one important thing, one meaningful thing, he thought. *And here it is.*

They seemed like good kids. Abby and David were both strung-out on terror, but they were handling it well. They were showing the sort of elasticity you seemed to lose after you hit thirty or even twenty and things got cemented in for the duration.

Abby seemed to be in charge of them.

She was like a mother bird with Megan and Denny. Sixteen years old and her parental instincts were beyond those of most women—and men—he'd ever known. They were using candles now, hoping not to attract too much attention and Tommy was amazed how the practicalities of babysitting had not abandoned her. After she changed little Megan's diaper, she cradled her in the crook of her arm and gave her a bottle. Denny was not left out. She had David go into the kitchen and get food and drinks. He returned with bottled water, bread, cheese, and cold cuts. She made sure that Denny ate and got some water into him.

Then it was a matter of waiting.

Tommy was worrying about a lot of things but mostly the fire because far in the distance, the town was burning. He kept hoping it would maybe burn itself out, but it was getting closer all the time.

"It can't be the whole world, can it?" David asked him. "I mean, those things can't be everywhere, can they?"

"I doubt it. We need to wait until dawn. When we get some light out there we'll be able to get a better idea of what's going on."

"I guess."

"We'll keep watch all night, it's all we can do."

The whole world. Now that hadn't really occurred to him before, but now that it had it left him cold. What if he had just become father figure and guardian protector of these kids not just for a few hours but days and weeks and months?

No, he wasn't going to worry about that.

He posted David by the front window to keep an eye out for action, then he went into the kitchen and watched the back yard. He lit a cigarette and found a bottle of Jack Daniels in the cupboard, but decided against it. He didn't need the kids smelling booze on him.

That's one right decision, he told himself. *Now keep going.*

About five minutes after he finished his smoke, he noticed that the air blowing in from outside was unpleasantly warm. So warm that he was beginning to sweat. It was weird, unseasonable.

David came in. "I want to show you something," he whispered.

Tommy had a good idea that he didn't want to see it, but he followed David back into the living room. At the picture window, he peered out into the night.

"You see it?"

"Yeah."

The blue glow to the north of them was very close now. Maybe just a few streets over, it seemed. It flickered irregularly, but it was always there. And just behind it, he could see the flickering light of the fire itself closing in.

"What should we do?" David wanted to know.

"We wait and see. There's nothing else we *can* do. We all need to rest right now. We can't keep running. In a little while, we'll get moving again."

That seemed to satisfy him, but it didn't satisfy Tommy himself. That glow scared him. Scared him bad because it was getting warmer.

44

Melody was pretty much tapped out and for a few scary moments there as she leaned against a fence, she couldn't even remember how any of this had come to be. Then it came back to her: Tiddles and Bobby Pistera. How long ago had that been? Four hours? Five? It was hard to know and even harder to think straight.

She was done in and she knew it.

She started walking again, away from the burning zones, as she now referred to them, but even here, many blocks away from the fires, the air was hot and smoky. Sweat ran down her face, stinging her eyes, and she felt a dizziness whirl in her head. It put her down to her knees. Her stomach jumped and flopped and as she put her hands down to steady herself, the burns on her palms cried out.

You're not going to make it much farther, lady, and you know it.

Bullshit.

She wasn't about to give in. Not after all this. She would keep going until she was out of town, until she hit the farms and fields and the encroaching woods. Then she'd follow the river to civilization.

She walked on another fifteen minutes until her legs went out from under her and even then she did not give in—she crawled. On her hands and knees, she crawled. In the end, all that mattered was forward momentum and she had that, by God.

45

Abby was sitting in the rocking chair by the fireplace, Megan snoozing in her arms and Denny racked out on the sofa, when she heard something thump against the outside of the house.

"Did you hear that?" she whispered, wiping sweat from her brow.

"Yeah," David said.

She set Megan down in the center of a little nest of blankets she had made for her. The air in the house had become positively stagnant with heat. Not the humidity of summer, but a sort of dry, desert heat.

She joined David and Tommy at the window.

They—all of them—were so close to that glowing now, perhaps near the very epicenter of it, that she could not really see it. It was more of a bluish mist in the air.

"Look," David said. "They're here."

And they were, Abby realized with a shudder. There were four of the zombie things out in the street. She could see them plainly enough, just not enough to tell whether they were men or women. They weren't doing anything, just standing there still as posts.

Tommy took off and came back about thirty seconds later. "There's more of them in the backyard out near the alley. Just standing there."

Abby had a great desire to start crying. She had been dealing with this nightmare for hours now and it just never seemed to end. How long could she hope to put on a brave face when she was scared white inside?

"You okay?" David said, gripping her hand.

She wanted to laugh. "No, I'm not okay, but I'll get by."

And really, what else was there?

The three of them waited there by the window, watching. It seemed every time they blinked their eyes or looked away, there were a couple more out there. If they would have moved or something, it wouldn't have been so unbelievably creepy. It was like the house was surrounded by mannequins. They just stood stock-still like they were waiting for orders.

There was no getting past the fact that it was getting even warmer in the house. They had no access to a thermometer but Abby was willing to bet it was in the mid-nineties and climbing. Her shirt was stuck to her back. Sweat kept pooling under her eyes and beading her face like dew. She could taste the salt of it on her lips.

They're bringing it, she thought then. *They must be.*

It seemed logical. She had never been too close to any of them, but close enough to feel the heat they created and there was no doubt that they incinerated anyone they touched. Maybe they were creating a sort of temperature inversion like she'd studied in Physical Science last year—a warm air mass that trapped the cooler air above.

Which means if enough of them gather out there, we're going to fry.

Tommy seemed to know a few things, but was very vague about his sources. He seemed to think the creatures were radioactive, emitting some exotic form of radiation but "not the radiation we know" as he said. That was disturbing. She wasn't so much worried about herself or David, but Megan and Denny. If radiation screwed-up their chromosomes—

"Something's happening," Tommy said.

And something certainly was.

More of them had gathered and she was guessing the number was up above fifty or sixty now if not closer to a hundred. In the misty moonlight, she could see them standing in ranks. They were swarming now like hornets, ghostly forms that threw out flickering blue-white auras that snapped and crackled. They were igniting, steam and smoke pouring from them, motes of burning dust rising from them like fireflies.

The temperature was spiking.

Sweat wasn't just beading on Abby's face now, it was running like tears. Dripping off her nose and chin. Her hair was wet with it. Both Tommy and David were down to their t-shirts now.

"I'm hot," Denny said, waking up.

She went to him and unzipped him out of his Dr. Denton's. His flesh was hot and greasy.

"Why's it so hot?" he asked.

"I don't know," she lied.

She went over to the window and, amazingly, it was even hotter over there. They were directing their heat against the house. She hoped it was only heat and not radioactivity. She touched a finger to the glass. It was so hot she jerked it away.

"They're gonna cook us," David said.

"Stop it," she told him.

She understood the need to freak out, she was very close to the edge herself, but for the sake of Denny and baby Megan it could not be allowed.

Megan began to thrash in her sleep.

Abby went to her and unzipped her out of her mint suit and down to her Onesie. Her skin was so warm it felt like she was baking. Abby used a hand towel to dab the sweat from her.

"They're moving," Tommy said.

Abby didn't need to be told that because the flickering was getting brighter and brighter now as if dozens of strobe lights were outside the window. But the glow seemed to be fading somehow and then she saw why—the heat. The glass was smudging with dark streaks from the heat being directed at it.

"Get back," Tommy told David.

And not a moment too soon because hands came reaching through the window, seven or eight of them burning their way right through as if their atoms had mixed with the atoms of glass. The hands were wild and clutching, trying to grab onto something. They were dead white things with erupted blisters and pustules, iridescent wounds that bled spokes of blue radiance, fingers blazing and sputtering, putting out twisting plumes of smoke.

Denny screamed and Megan woke up again, crying her eyes out. Abby tried to calm them both with David's help, but they were beyond comfort.

A face came through the smoke-stained glass. A pallid cadaver face with the texture of toad flesh, holes punched through it like somebody had been pounding spikes into it. Its mouth was a puckered galvanic hole, the hollow pits of its eyes sparking and hissing like electrical sockets.

One of the hands found a drape and ripped it down, the drape itself mushrooming with flames. Everything those hands touched was burned or scalded.

Tommy brought up his gun and put two rounds into the face, opening up more holes that emitted more of the glaring, blinding illumination that cooked inside it.

"The basement!" David cried. "We'll be safe in the basement!"

Abby shook her head, coughing on the heat and fumes. "We'll be trapped," she said.

But she didn't see why it would really matter because they were trapped right now. They were Hansel and Gretel in the witch's oven and she was slowing closing the door on them.

46

The windows were gone now. They had literally fallen apart. And out there, Tommy could see the fire-eaters. The ones closest to the house wanted to get in, but hadn't decided just yet what the best way of doing that was.

But even the immediate threat they presented did not interest him.

It was the others, the scores of others standing out in the street that he was watching and what he was seeing was simply beyond reason. They were standing stiffly out there, shaking and trembling and as he saw them in the lights of burning cars and burning hedges, he saw a peculiar thing happen—they began to blacken and crisp, their hides splitting open in spider-webbed cracks until he could clearly see the oxidizing blue energy pulsing within.

And then...

And then he saw them split open, giving birth to white shimmering orbs that spread feelers out into the air around them. As he watched, dozens of the orbs were born from the smoking refuse of the fire-eaters. They pulsated and drifted in the sky, their feelers fanning out, purple-blue electricity branching out from them into myriad webs of electrified plasma.

They were far too bright to look directly at.

They floated out there like crystal balls, white-hot and smoking, their filament-like tendrils sparking with high voltage. Everything around them—houses, trees, bushes—burst into flame.

They hadn't yet started moving at the house, but they would.

"Get back!" Tommy told the others. *"Get into the dining room with the little ones!"*

The heat was pouring into the room now and his face felt so hot it was as if his blood was coming to a boil. His arms felt like they were seared with the worst sunburn he had ever known. But it wasn't just that; it was inside him, too, fiery and eruptive. It felt like hundred of white-hot needles were piercing him like pins in a voodoo doll.

Abby and David were standing frozen there at the dining room door, perplexed and shocked and he turned and screamed at them to get the kids inside. It was their only protection.

"Move! MOVE!"

They did as he instructed.

The sliding doors of the dining room slid shut. He could hear Denny and the baby crying in there as more and more hands burned through the window. But they weren't just there but at the door now, too. He could hear them knocking and pounding. Smoke was rising from the door's face, the little windows at the top blackened and fell apart. The knob and lock were superheating. The door was cracking, blue light spilling through. Now the paint was bubbling and blistering, actually liquefying from the heat and running in globules.

He had no plan.

He had no idea what to do.

As the door cracked open, more of that spiking blue light came through and when it hit him, he cried out. It was like being an ant under a magnifying glass.

The air was so heavy and hot it was nearly unbreathable. It was burning in his throat and lungs, like trying to draw a breath in the scorching fumes from a coke oven. He began to feel dizzy and disoriented. His guts felt like they were on fire. His arms were covered with nasty red blisters that ran with a foul-smelling puss.

Is this it? a voice called in his head. *Is this how you do something important and meaningful? Is this your final unselfish, significant act? To die a horrible death like a bug in a frying pan? Is this all you can come up with?*

But sadly, it was.

He could barely stay on his feet now, his head filled with expanding black dots. He began to cough out blood and one of his molars slid from its gum. He spat it out along with a whole lot of blood.

The door exploded off its melting hinges and the things were coming in, bringing waves of cremating heat and burning, gaseous fumes that made his vision blur.

No more, can't take any more.

But he forced himself to.

As one of them reached out its hands for him, he emptied the clip of the 9mm into it and each hole he opened up brought a searing ray of light that burned into him and made him cry out. The thing came on, smoldering like a melting fission core, exhaling superhot gases that speared through him like irradiated subatomic particles.

One of the fire-eaters reached out and grabbed his wrist and its fingers were like white-hot seams of radium.

He yanked his hand away…only he no longer had a hand but a blackened stump with a couple of bones sticking out of it. This was it. Endgame. He'd done all he could and there was no escape—

Wait.

Something was happening.

The house was vibrating and shaking. Things were falling off shelves. He heard a window break and something else pitch over and crash.

The orbs were coming.

47

In the dining room, Abby could see a blinding white light coming under the door, but that didn't concern her as much as the sounds—a strange, sharp sort of crackling coming in from outside and a whirring that was nearly a high-pitched squealing. It reminded her of a buzzsaw cutting through steel plating.

David's face was pallid in the light. "What the hell is that?"

"I don't know."

"It's getting louder."

"Yes."

Both Denny and Megan were crying now at the top of their lungs and they were completely beyond comforting much as Abby was herself.

But as loud as they were, they were practically a whisper compared to what was coming in from outside and making the entire house shake. The whirring and the crackling got louder and louder until they became an immense wall of noise, a solid ear-jarring, bone-jangling sound like the steady drone of a dentist's drill amplified to deafening levels.

David was shouting something but Abby could not be sure what it was. The light coming under the door was not diminishing but increasing and they knew Tommy was going through a living hell out there but there wasn't a damn thing they could do to help him.

She felt something grab her arm and she nearly went wild in that evil cacophony, but it was only David tugging her towards the window in the dining room. There were black streaks on its outer surface, but they were minor because it hadn't taken the directed heat of the windows in the living room.

"WHAT?" she shouted, her voice barely audible.

He pointed out the window. "LOOK!" he mouthed.

Abby, sweating and shaking and nearly delirious by that point, put her face up to the glass and saw...she wasn't quite sure. Glowing balls bouncing in the night? No, not exactly that. The house they were in was on a corner and the street moved casually downhill so it gave her a fairly wide-angle view of the town below.

And just above the treetops and rooflines, she saw phosphorescent ghostly spheres of some sort that were bright white and blinding like miniature suns. They shimmered with heat waves like a blacktop road at high summer.

Despite the noise around her—which seemed to be lessening now so that she could actually hear Denny whimpering and Megan wailing—she watched the spheres with morbid fascination the way the characters in *War of the Worlds* had watched the coming of the Martian war machines. She couldn't stop watching them even though she very much sensed her own destruction in their approach.

"What the hell are they?" she heard David say.

She could only shake her head. She had no idea what they were, but her mind went back to Physical Science again when they had watched a video of the sun ejecting hot blobs of plasma into space. Whether there was a correlation between the two, she did not know.

The spheres were pulsating, plumes of white smoke twisting up from them. They had branching tendrils moving out from either side and they moved with a lazy, sluggish, almost rhythmic motion like deep sea grasses in the gentle pull of a current.

As the spheres drifted slowly forward, they cast an intense radiance before them that turned night not to day but something far beyond day, something much more brilliant that would have burned out your retinas if you viewed it too closely. As the spheres moved, they must have been putting out an ungodly amount of heat. The sort you might acquaint with the guts of a reactor core. Trees burst into flame, rooftops exploded into fiery kindling, telephone poles and church steeples blazed like struck kitchen matches.

It was incredible.

And it was horrible because they were heading towards the house. She saw one of them, what seemed a very large one, move over the rounded dome of city hall which flared up in a white eruption of fire and smoke like burning phosphorous. Judging by the size of the dome, the sphere had to be at least a hundred feet across. The others were smaller, some considerably so, but no less destructive as they spread a searing firestorm in all directions.

We can't stand up against that, Abby thought. *We can't survive something like that.*

As things ignited in the distance, they could feel the rolling vibrations of their explosions. It was like echoing thunder.

The whining outside the house had lessened some, but it was still loud, a constant electric humming that made the silver service in the dining room buffet cabinet rattle like dice in a cup.

Abby picked up Megan and held her tightly as David took Denny by the hand and the amazing thing was that the children had now gone quiet as if they, too, sensed the end and were ready to meet it.

"We need to get out of here," she said.

David shook his head. "To where?" His face was shiny with sweat, his mouth hooked in a grimace that belonged on a much older face, and his eyes were huge and filled with a terror that he could not put into words.

Abby went over to the window and saw that the spheres had reached the park now and all those stately, majestic elm trees that lined Shady Lane and rose well over a hundred feet in height were burning. Although they were essentially just trees, they had always been something she loved in Middleburg. All of them were well over a hundred years old and had survived the ravages of Dutch Elm disease that had destroyed countless others across the country in the 20th century. Now they were burning. Not just burning, but falling like tall timber, crashing into one another, splitting open and shattering from the incredible heat.

And the spheres continued on, engulfing neighborhood after neighborhood in flames.

Time was running out.

In ten or fifteen minutes, they would be here.

Abby felt tears roll down her sweaty face and she could not seem to stop them.

48

Barely able to draw a breath in the oven of spiraling smoke and heat, Tommy stumbled over to the door of the dining room, pounding on it with his one good hand and leaving a smear of blood on it. "GET OUTSIDE! GET OUTSIDE! RUN FOR GODSAKE! THEY'RE COMING—"

Whether they heard him or not, he could not say. He heard Abby cry out and maybe David, too. Tommy knew he had done all he could and as he turned around, three of the fire-eaters took him. They reached out and grabbed him and he screamed with a raw hysteria as the agony tore him apart inside.

When they seized him, their fingers were like hot scalpels cutting into him. He actually heard his flesh sizzle like bacon and could—if only for a moment—smell the stink of his own charred meat. His awareness dropped by degrees after that and it was like plunging down, down into the deepest, blackest well imaginable and it was a relief, an absolute relief.

Embraced by the things, his body swelled up like a corpse decomposing in direct sunlight. His muscles, tendons, and ligaments snapped their housings as his face opened up with red blisters that popped like bubbles and his brain became a pressure cooker of heat and steam, his eyes liquefying and running down his face in a stringy discharge.

By then, of course, his insides were oxidizing, becoming a steaming liquid polymer that reached the boiling point, gurgling and bubbling from the skeleton below, vomitous gouts of tissue erupting in hot geysers as he sank in an effervescent sea of red jelly that gushed and flooded its banks.

What was left of him hit the floor as a blazing skeleton, but nobody was there to see it and that was probably a good thing.

49

From her vantage point on a hilltop, Melody watched the destruction of the town; she watched Middleburg become ground zero in hell. She couldn't understand any of it much as she tried, so she stopped trying and just stared with awe in her eyes as if she were watching a Fourth of July fireworks display.

The orbs moved over the town, sentient blowtorches whose sulfur breath made it burn, made huge clouds of red, yellow, and orange flames leap into the night as houses were incinerated to hot glowing coals and bricks crumbled, glass went liquid and steel frameworks became putty. The inferno, not just a fire now but a living angry fire god, spread its cremating wings horizon to horizon, eating its way forward with brimstone teeth, setting all and everything ablaze in a fiery cauldron of rising sparks and crackling embers and immense boiling clouds of smoke that darkened the sky in mushrooming masses. Still, the living furnace was not satisfied and it continued to march, burning everything, glutting itself on the fuel of Middleburg, greedy to sink its teeth into the surrounding forests and farmland in a monstrous, apocalyptic conflagration.

Although Melody could not see what the fires left in their wake because of the churning smoke, she could pretty much imagine that the town looked like a fire pit of blackened cinders and blowing gray ash that blew in whirlwinds and cyclones of powdery, dirty snow. The spheres left behind a fire-gutted corpse and little else.

Are you going to stand here and wait for them or are you going to leave?

The rational thing was to run but she didn't have much energy left for that. It seemed that simply staying on her feet took everything that she had. Burned and sooty, she just stood there watching the town burn inch by terrible inch, thinking of the firestorms that followed the bombings of Dresden and Tokyo in World War II. The night resounded with explosions and crashing noises beneath the spreading curtain of flames.

She watched the spheres.

They continued on, seemingly drawn by the heat, maybe feeding off the released energy of the mass burning they had created. Fire released carbon dioxide, she knew, and maybe that was what they wanted and maybe it was nothing that logical. Maybe they simply wanted to spend their wrath and create death and destruction.

Down there, directly in the path of the spheres she could see a veritable army of the fire-starters. They were also moving in her direction. Some of them split open and released more orbs that rose into the night like balloons, but others were bathed in the light of the orbs and simply ignited, their remains drawn up to be absorbed.

There was a gas station down there and the heat found it. The station went up and then the tanks themselves with a roaring that shook the town as immense fire-clouds rose spinning into the sky.

The spheres were getting closer and she could feel their awful heat hitting her in waves, but still she did not move.

She just waited for the end.

Yet, her mind did not want it to end. It wanted her to escape and live and maybe, more importantly, it wanted to understand all this if it could be understood at all. So, standing there, the heat of the orbs on her now like direct July sunshine and getting hotter, she forced her brain to reason. *Bobby Pistera.* Yes, Bobby. He was probably the only witness to the beginning of it. What had he said? God, it was so long ago. Like trying to remember the plot of a movie she'd seen years before. *Think.* Yes, she remembered. Hail. Bobby said something about hail falling that wasn't like any hail he had ever seen, shiny hail. Then he said people were screaming. And some guy was walking around with his hair on fire. She connected that, of course, with the shards in her garage that seemed to attack Bobby, changing him into one of those things.

Logic dictated that the hail was the shards. They had fallen from the sky. *They came from outer space.* They fell and attacked people, turned them into those things which in turn were just hosts for the orbs. Like some insane life cycle. But it all started with the shards. She would never know what they were or where they came from.

But they were what started this.

Sighing, sweat running down her face as the orbs got closer, she had to block their light with her hand.

She thought that now was the time to run before it was too late...but run where? If those shards, crystals, whatever the hell they were had fallen everywhere, then this could be a global thing. Is that what she wanted to live for? To become a rat scrambling from one ash pile to the next as the orbs lit the world on fire?

There could really be no escape.

The towns and cities would be burned flat, the fields lit on fire, the forests blazing down to blackened sticks, the rivers and lakes boiled to steam. Even the oceans would go sooner or later. All that would be left was a blackened pyre blown by ashes. Even the atmosphere would be burned away sooner or later. The Earth would become what it was in the beginning, billions of years ago in the Archaeozic—a blasted, burnt netherworld whose crust was cracked open, immense lava flows gushing over the land, the atmosphere poisoned by toxic gases.

With that in mind, Melody waited for it.

Waited for the end.

She knew it wouldn't be long in coming.

50

Abby and the others had heard Tommy and they wasted no time. While he was still under attack, David opened the door that led into the kitchen and Abby followed with the children. Had they gotten out there twenty seconds later, it would have been far too late because the things were already melting their way through the windows and the door leading outside.

Denny was wailing and Megan was crying and it was pandemonium on every level.

"GO! GO! GO!" Abby shouted at David as he hesitated to look at what was outside the window.

He led them away out of the kitchen and down a hallway that cut to the west side of the house. By then, the things that had cooked Tommy were already filling the kitchen and in hot pursuit. Maybe they couldn't see, but they could hear just fine and the cacophony the children were putting out drew them on.

David selected a bedroom at the back because it had a large window looking out into the backyard. He hustled Abby and the children in there as the things filled the hallway. They were superheating now and he could see the pulsing blue cores inside each that were reaching critical mass as they split open.

As he slammed the door shut, two of them reached for him and their hands got caught between the door and the jamb. He kept ramming it shut until one hand retreated and the other was trapped. He forced the door shut and the wiggling fingers of the creature outside exploded like hot fuses with a crackling sound.

"Hurry, David!" Abby said. "The window!"

The door secured, he ran over there and started kicking it but it did not shatter the way he figured it would so he picked up a chair and swung it with everything he had, cracks appearing in the glass. He swung it again until it shattered completely.

Abby was watching the door.

The paint was blistering in rising bubbles, the knob smoking, and the door itself beginning to split open.

David crawled out the window and Abby set Megan on the bed and handed Denny out to him, being careful not to cut him on shards of glass sticking out from the frame. Then she handed him Megan and crawled out herself.

They got out just in time as the orbs in the front moved at the house. The roof went up first, the shingles exploding into flames, fire filling the attic and rushing down hallways in a storm of red sparks. The house crackled and split, falling into itself as the heat tore it asunder, vomiting ashes and embers into the night. The fire was like a million writhing orange-red snakes. The house shook, shuddering on its black bones, scalded and seared and gutted, and came down in a raging blizzard of flames.

Abby and David got the kids well away from it, but there was little else they could do. Sweltering in the heat, they sank to the ground, overcome by smoke and fumes. The fire-eaters came for them as the orbs grew closer and closer and the air became trembling hot gelatin. They were burning superhot, charged with unstable elements.

Then something happened.

Whether it was the intervention of a higher power or simply fate or coincidence, something happened.

It started to rain.

In fact, it poured. The rain came down in gray sheets and fires went out and yards filled with water and streets began to flood.

In the noise and heat and confusion, Abby's brain which was baking away in the pan of her skull like a well-seasoned rib roast, did not recognize it for what it was. A storm. A rainstorm. More so, an absolute fucking downpour, the kind flash floods are born of.

It was the most natural thing in this world and the most deadly thing for those who came from a dry, hot, and possibly blazing world of noxious steam and burning smoke.

The fire-eaters were getting drenched and the result was amazing, absolutely amazing.

It was like acid.

Abby screeched her joy. *Yes! Yes! Goddamn fucking yes!* a voice cried from deep inside her, triumphant and invincible.

Raindrops hit them and burned holes right through them. It drilled into them like bullets.

The fire-eaters' flesh was cheesecloth, tearing and rupturing and turning to rivers of molten flesh-goo. Faces went liquid, bubbling drainage that splashed off the skulls beneath. The flickering lights inside them were extinguished like candles. They stumbled about, tangled in their own gooey anatomies, strings of flesh hanging from their fingers, tissue sluicing in undulant webs of flesh.

They weren't very smart because they did not even try to get out of the rain. All they did was stumble about in circles.

Abby saw a woman and the rain cut trenches through her white cadaverous face. She held her hands up to stop it, but it burned right through them. She staggered away, her face squirming, it seemed, like some wriggling amoebal mass, liquefying and running from the skull in loops of ropy tissue. She glared out with flayed red sockets, her flesh gone to bubbling wax that hung in strings.

A man near her let out a shrill hissing cry as his skin blackened and crisped, the light snuffed inside him, his gurgling red liquid center pouring out like melted plastic right before he exploded with a cracking sound.

It was happening to all of them.

Abby and the others crept out of the downfall and huddled beneath the branches of an oak tree and watched it happen.

The things were everywhere.

A little girl dissolved into a slime of white gore that hissed in the grass. A man stumbled towards them, holding his head in fleshless hands. His face went to hot liquid latex and squirted between his fingers. Several others melted into one central mass of bubbling corpse-fat that oozed in the yard.

It was the same all across Middleburg.

The things were in the streets and yards, on the sidewalks and in vacant lots and empty fields, all of them going slowly to the earth in a sludge of tissue, steaming flesh, and hot marrow that erupted from rent bones and sizzled in the rain. Decomposition was fairly quick and within fifteen minutes, the creatures that had laid waste to the town no longer existed. Their bones were everywhere, scattered and broken and split open, skulls cracked apart like hot chestnuts.

But this was the only testament to their having ever existed. The fires slowly began to go out, leaving a blackened, fire-gutted ruin in their wake. And the architects of it all, the immense orbs, began to die, too. If it wasn't death, then it was simple nonexistence. Steaming and sputtering, their luminous white masses began to gray and thread with minute black cracks. One by one, they fell to earth like deflating hot air balloons. They hissed and steamed and spluttered, their tendrils withering to black arid roots that dissolved to an inky fluid. Each and every one of them went out like light bulbs with broken filaments and as they did, they went rubbery and sloughing, caving-in and collapsing. They blackened into sludge that the rain washed away in dirty streams.

Sitting under the tree, holding Megan and being held by Denny and David, Abby heard sirens in the distance. The world was still out there then. Emergency crews were on the move. It was a good sign.

"Goobdub," Megan said, blinking dramatically in the rain.

Someone came walking through the yard and Abby saw it was a woman in bathrobe. She was soaking wet, her face reddened with what looked like the worst sunburn she'd ever seen. The woman was bruised and limping, but she managed a thin smile, sitting down next to Abby and pulling her knees up to her chest.

"Is it going to be okay now?" Abby asked her.

The woman put an arm around her and pulled her close, smiling down at Megan. "Yes. Yes, I think it will be."

Together, they waited.

—The End—